"Twin beds," Emily said with a smile.

"I'd tease you about having twin beds in your room…if I were to stay."

She couldn't guess what Ryan was thinking; his expression was closed to her. "They've always been in this room," he said.

"But haven't you thought of getting a more comfortable—" Emily stopped herself, embarrassed. It sounded as if she was obsessed with beds.

Ryan propped his feet on the wooden table, leaned back and at last he smiled. "I thought about it, but maybe I just never had the right incentive." He gave her a long, smoldering look. "Are you saying my bed was too small last night?"

There was no fighting the sensations of desire that overcame her at the thought of making love with him. Now that she knew him, knew his body, his moans of pleasure, his mesmerizing eyes, she couldn't help herself, no more now than she could last night.

"Emily…" he whispered. "Tonight… Come tonight…." His voice trailed off, and when he kissed her she knew that whether he wanted to want her or not, he did—passionately.

The setting of *Twin Beds* is the view from the windows of the hundred-year-old farmhouse in Brown County, Indiana, which **Regan Forest** and her husband have recently renovated. Their wooded acres are shared by their two dogs—a mastiff and a shepherd mix named Sanders— who charmed his way into this story. The lake behind the farmhouse is lined with cattails and wild roses and surrounded by groves of trees. Regan insists that the little island in their lake— Pillywiggin—is enchanted, and it was yet another inspiration for this story.

Books by Regan Forest

Don't miss any of our special offers. Write to us at the following address for information on our newest releases.

Harlequin Reader Service
U.S.: 3010 Walden Ave., P.O. Box 1325, Buffalo, NY 14269
Canadian: P.O. Box 609, Fort Erie, Ont. L2A 5X3

TWIN BEDS
REGAN FOREST

Harlequin Books

**TORONTO • NEW YORK • LONDON
AMSTERDAM • PARIS • SYDNEY • HAMBURG
STOCKHOLM • ATHENS • TOKYO • MILAN
MADRID • WARSAW • BUDAPEST • AUCKLAND**

To my husband, Bill, who has shown me that happy endings are even more beautiful in real life than in dreams....

ISBN 0-373-25691-4

TWIN BEDS

Copyright © 1996 by Regan Forest.

Printed in U.S.A.

Prologue

CHIGGER BALANCED the dull, round rock in his hand to test its weight and announced that he was holding something magical. Emily, bewildered, watched breathlessly while he pounded the rock with a hammer.

Just when she was beginning to think he was playing a trick on her, the rock broke in half. Inside, lavender and silver crystals sparkled in the sun. If one looked closely, it was easy to imagine it was a tiny, hidden cathedral, just the size for fairies. Emily drew in her breath and laughed with delight.

The boy held out the pieces, one in each hand. "This is the best half," he said. "It's yours."

"You mean to keep?" Fifteen-year-old Emily accepted the gift with her heart pounding. "How could you have known it had such magic inside? It looked like any other old rock to me!"

"They're called geodes," Chigger said. "I find them around here sometimes. I can tell one when I—" The boy stopped abruptly and touched her hand. "Listen! Your uncles's tractor! Heading this way. Duck!"

They crouched low, hidden by the treasures of an unmowed meadow—Queen Anne's lace, yarrows, mare's tails and meadow rues. Emily felt the heat of

Chigger's body next to hers in the midday summer sun. "I'll bet Uncle Leo's looking for me," she whispered. "I was supposed to be back a half hour ago. If he sees me with you, I'll really get it."

"If he ever did anything to you, *he'd* really get it," the boy vowed with his jaw clenched tight.

Emily looked at him with surprised curiosity. "You're barely seventeen. What could you do to him?"

"I've done lots of things to him. I've put mud in his gas tank and a potato in his exhaust pipe—"

She stared at this mysterious boy who lived across the meadow, a boy she had met three days after arriving at Appleyard Farm to visit her aunt and uncle. He was the cutest guy she had ever seen and by far the most daring. She wanted to be with him every minute, in spite of strict warnings to stay away from Wildwood and not set one foot on Callister land.

Chigger was laughing. "You shoulda seen it. When Leo started up his truck and the pipe got hot, that potato shot out like a rocket and smashed a hole in his garden trellis. You shoulda heard him yell."

The mental picture made her smile. "But why did you do it? Why do your family and mine hate each other so much?"

"Because his father tried to steal our land a long time ago." His pale blue eyes turned the color of a dark lake. "But I hate him because he tries to shoot my dog if he runs over there. He's a mean old man, mean as the devil."

"I think he's mean, too," she said. "But I like my aunt Eve. She's my mom's sister, so it's not like Uncle Leo is a real relative, by blood or anything."

"I'm glad of that." He smiled, his eyes shining blue again, and fixed on hers. She watched the shadows of wildflowers dance on his face as she clutched the geode he had given her. He gazed at her eyes as though he were seeing some remarkable secret and she couldn't look away, not before he leaned forward and kissed her cheek, then her lips, lightly and tenderly. A fuzzy, giddy feeling came over her, and she thought, *my first real kiss!* as she reeled at the wonder of being in love.

He offered his hand as he got to his feet. "Come on, Miss Emily Rose. You might get bit by a big chigger if you sit in the grass any longer." This was his idea of a joke and she giggled all the way back to the fence, where he held the barbed wire open for her to climb through. Several times he looked back over his shoulder, and she wondered why, because he couldn't have been looking for Uncle Leo, whose tractor was heading back toward the barn.

Chigger stood by the fence, knowing Emily would turn back once with a small wave as she ran toward the Appleyard farmhouse. He waved back, then headed in the direction of home, over a path worn by deer. He was thinking about the fresh clean smell of her hair and the feel of her soft cheek against his. When their dog ran out to meet him, he knew his brother wasn't far away. The other boy, his mirror image, came out from behind a clump of trees, protesting loudly.

"No fair! You were with her ever since lunch. It was my turn!"

"Can I help it if she likes me better?" He tossed up the geode and caught it, wondering why he was feeling so funny inside. He kept picturing the other half in Emily's pretty hand.

"She does not." His twin kicked up a cloud of dirt with his bare foot. "She likes *me* better! I'm going to take her over to Pillywiggin."

"No way. We agreed! It's private. Nobody goes there but us!" Even as he made the adamant protest, he was thinking, *If anybody takes Emily over to the island, it's going to be me.*

"Okay," his twin conceded. "But if she comes out after supper and nobody is sitting on their back porch to see her sneak away, it's my turn to talk to her."

Exchanging identities was a trick they had loved to play for as long as the twins could remember. Emily had no idea there were two of them who answered to the nickname Chigger. He felt some guilt about this, but with their "take turns" game in progress, he was guaranteed time alone with her, and he wanted that time alone, so he could kiss her again. The soft sensation of her lips on his was unlike anything he had ever imagined. He wanted very much to kiss her again.

THEY SAT ON THE SHORE a day later, dangling their feet in the water and looking out across the still lake and the reflections of the trees and sky. Emily asked, "What's on that island? Do you ever go there?"

"Yeah. It's a magic place, enchanted. Even my mom says so. She says fairies live there."

Her eyes grew wide. "A magic place? Oh, Chigger, please take me! I want to see it! Please! How do you get over there?"

"A raft." He dug his bare toes into the cool grass. "If we go over there, it'll have to be late at night when nobody would see us. We'll have to sneak out of the house. At midnight."

She gasped. "In the dark?"

"It won't be dark tonight. There's a full moon and no clouds."

Emily squirmed with excitement. He was so *fearless!* "Oh, would I *dare?*"

Chigger turned his blue eyes on her and smiled his handsome smile that dimpled his right cheek, and it no longer mattered how much of a risk it was. She'd be there.

His shoulder brushed hers. "It's really neat, but I don't ever take anybody else over to Pillywiggin— that's what my mom named the island. It's a special kind of secret place."

She reached for a tall-stemmed wild daisy and broke it off, and it took all her willpower to resist tickling his dimple with the soft flower. "Then how come I get to see it?"

His face became somber. He took the flower from her and, as if he had been reading her mind, tickled the end of her nose with it. "Because I like you."

His words were clouds falling, covering her with soft, cottony mist and sparkles of light. Emily shivered with happiness. "I like you, too," she said, dropping her gaze timidly.

"Will you meet me tonight?"

Her heart fluttered. "Okay," she agreed. "I'll sneak out."

"Great!" he said. "Wear dark clothes. And don't let anybody hear you. Especially your uncle."

"He won't. He's always passed out drunk by ten o'clock. Aunt Eve goes to bed real early. My mom even goes to bed early since we've been here. She says it's the country air." Emily paused, hesitating. She splashed water with her feet, sending sparkles into the sunshine. "But, Chigger...the thing is...don't snakes come out at night?"

He considered this. Emily was from the city, after all. And even country girls always thought about crawly things. He smiled. "Instead of you meeting me out here, I'll come up to the porch and wait for you by the house." He touched her arm. "Don't worry, Emily. I'll be with you. Nothing is ever gonna hurt you as long as you're with me."

RETURNING HOME with her heart singing, Emily was surprised to see her mother's car in the driveway with the doors open and a suitcase outside. In the farmhouse, tension was so high, Emily entered the kitchen with trepidation. Only Aunt Eve and her mother were there, and her mother's face was ashen. Something awful must have happened!

"Emily," her mother said. "You've been gone since early morning. Where have you been?"

"Just out hiking around, Mom. Why? What's wrong?"

"Our plans have changed. We're leaving. I've already packed. Please pack your things as quickly as you can."

Aunt Eve sat red-eyed and silent at the table. Emily sensed whatever was wrong had to do with Uncle Leo.

"We can't leave now, Mom!" she wailed. "We're supposed to be here another week!"

"We are leaving, and immediately." Her mother's voice sounded different; the decision was not negotiable.

Always one to be straightforward with her daughter, Emily's mother opened up on the way home. In a choking voice, she explained. "Leo Stark is a terrible man. This morning in the greenhouse, he made a pass at me. A serious pass, the lech! I won't have either of us in that house with him. We won't go back there ever again!"

Ever again! The words echoed in every beat of Emily's pulse. *Ever again ...*

EYES BURNING WITH TEARS, she sat in her room, hours away in Chicago, watching the clock's minute hand move closer to midnight. The full moon was visible from her window. She clutched her precious geode in her hand.

The pain in her heart deepened with each passing second. *He's waiting for me by the porch. But I won't be there. Not ever again.*

1

Ten years later

THE SQUEAK of Aunt Eve's rocking chair on such a lazy summer day might have put Emily to sleep, had her mind not been so preoccupied with memories. Gazing down toward the lake, she could see the tops of the trees on the island at the far end. Pillywiggin, he had called it. The lake was L-shaped. The property line was at the bend of the L, with the largest area of water on Callister land. The smaller, fatter portion was part of Stark's Appleyard Farm. But the lake couldn't be crossed, not ten years ago, and not now, because Leo had strung a barbed-wire barrier across the water.

"It's so good of you to come," Aunt Eve said, fanning herself with a magazine as she sipped a tall glass of orange juice.

Emily looked away from the misty view of the island, to the meadows, dotted with shade trees casting their wide shadows, and woods behind the meadows on every side. It was so green here, so beautiful. How could a place be so beautiful? She said, "I've wanted to come back for years. But I couldn't, with Uncle Leo here."

Eve stopped fanning. "My dear, you don't know how I suffered over that. Every time I went to Chicago to visit your mother and you, there was hell to pay when I got home. I don't think that man said a kind word to me for the last twenty years of his profane and wicked life." She shook her head. "I know you think I should have left him. Believe me, I wanted to, but I was too afraid of him." She brushed back a wisp of silver hair and smiled with more abandon than Emily had ever seen from her dainty little aunt. "Emily, I feel free for the first time since I was a girl."

Her niece smiled softly. "Are you okay financially, then?"

"Oh, yes. I have an offer on Leo's hardware business in Phantom Ridge Village, from a man who has wanted it for years and was already negotiating with Leo to buy him out. I'll be quite well-off."

The nicest thing he ever did for her was to die, Emily thought. And thank heaven it was before he had time to drink away what they had.

"I've come to dearly love the farm," Eve was saying. "And I'll never leave, but I will have to hire a man to keep it going for me. I'm a strong woman, but I can't do the work required to keep a place like this up, even if I don't farm any of it, which I won't. I'll keep some of the fields in hay to sell, and there's a nice yield from my fruit trees. I'll have my garden. I'll be very content."

Emily turned from the rail, helped herself to juice from the icy pitcher and plopped into the porch swing. The back porch, which stretched the length of the house, was wide and shady and furnished with white wicker furniture and countless pots of flowers. In warm weather there was a fresh white cloth on the porch table every morning. The swing's squeak played in rhythm with the rocking chair, familiar melody of a summer day in the hills of southern Indiana. Everything looked the same, smelled the same, sounded the same, tasted the same. A quick sip of cold juice hurt her temples, making her smile, remembering that, too.

He should be out there, across the meadow or on the lakeshore with his fishing pole. He should be out there waiting for her to sneak away into the woods or the high grass or behind the wall of cattails.

The fantasy hurt, for he would be a man by now—twenty-seven years old, he'd be. And probably with a wife and some adorable little kids with bright blue eyes. Emily wanted him back with such an ache...wanted to run across the meadow and into his arms, as she had in her million dreams. In all her twenty-five years, she had never found anyone else who made her fall helplessly in love, the way he did. Her first love. The boy she could never forget, or ever stop loving.

So involved was she in memories, it took Eve's words a long time to sink in: She had just said she needed help with the farm...needed help. Yes, of course, she would!

Emily began to swing vigorously, energized by the first sparks of an idea. Maybe she could help out for the rest of her summer vacation; after all, there were several weeks left with nothing planned except a tentative trip to California with her roommate, which she wasn't very keen on. Jennifer's pilot boyfriend lived there and Emily would feel like a third wheel whether they "fixed her up with her choice of his fellow pilots," as Jennifer had insisted, or not.

Though she had applied for another teaching job overseas and was still hoping a good offer would come before she had to sign her contract in Chicago, the checking could be done from here. Her legs stretched straight out in front of her—white legs, badly in need of a tan. She said, "I've got some time this summer, Aunt Eve. I'll stay and help out so you don't have to be in any big hurry hiring a guy."

Eve blinked and her mouth dropped open, as if to speak, but Emily wasn't finished. "I can drive the tractor mower and weed the garden...it'll be wonderful fun, and we'll enjoy some time together. Now that Mother's gone, you and I are the only family left...."

Eve's pale eyes flashed with joy. "I can't think of anything more wonderful! How long is your vacation?"

"I don't actually have to be back until mid-August, because I can fax in my signature when the contracts come out. I'm not even sure whether I'll be teaching in Chicago again this year." Her eyes scanned the branches of a nearby mulberry tree, looking for the robin who was singing. "I'm considering another job overseas next fall. England. One reason I wanted to be a teacher was so I could be mobile. I'm a gypsy, Aunt Eve. I have no roots anywhere. I'm as free as a bird."

"Stay as long as you like, Emily, and when you get restless again, you can go on to whatever adventures await you. For now, though, nothing could make me happier than for you to be here awhile with me."

Emily rose from the swing. "This is great! A summer in the country. I'd like to lay claim to the pink room with the view of the lake!"

Eve laughed. "You can have the entire upstairs. I've been using the downstairs bedroom so I won't have to climb the steps so much."

The upstairs was more space than Emily had ever had to live in. Spacious rooms filled with antiques and satin and lace curtains were timelessly beautiful under a layer of dust.

"I love this big old house," she said. "I used to like to wander through the rooms, and I was secretly thrilled when I got to stay in the pink room." She raised her glass in a salute. "Here's to our summer, Aunt Eve!"

Always the practical one, Eve asked, "Do you have enough clothes with you?"

"I have most of my summer clothes. I can't be burdened with too many material things in my pursuit of a gypsy life. I'll ask my roommate to pack up the rest of my jeans and shirts and send them down."

"You'll have to tell me more about your life, dear. I didn't know you had a roommate."

"Jennifer is a flight attendant who flies in and out of town. Sometimes I don't see her for days."

"But you want to give up your apartment and go to England?"

"Yes. I love England. It's so green." *Like here*, she thought. Emily glanced out over the green lawn that sloped down to the lake. Shadows of giant walnuts and sugar maples patterned the grass. Carefully tended flowers grew around the trees. To the right was the barn and greenhouse, its glass roof catching a bright glare of sun. I love Appleyard Farm, her thoughts were singing. She didn't know for how long, but for now, there was no place she would rather be!

Eve picked up the tray of orange juice and glasses and followed Emily into the house. "This calls for a celebration. I'm going to put party clothes on my geese."

"What?" Emily stopped, causing Eve to slam into the back of her with the tray. "*What* did you just say?"

"Party clothes. My geese. Right now they're wearing dark capes, but Leo's been dead for over a week. Mourning's over. I can dance in my own house again. You're here. Our new life begins. So...party clothes to celebrate!"

Oh, yes, Emily remembered—the ceramic geese on the front lawn. Many yards had them around here, and many of the geese were wearing costumes. Flowered bonnets, aprons, dresses, satin capes. Driving in, just a couple of hours ago, Emily had spotted some with Fourth of July outfits. One wore a coonskin cap, and another an Indiana sweatshirt, and another a two-piece bikini.

This was too good to miss. She followed Eve to the dining room and watched her choose from a collection of tiny clothes that filled a drawer of the big hutch.

"These are the best party clothes I've made," Eve boasted. "The sequins sparkle in the sun."

"They are adorable!" Emily sorted through the drawer, pulling out a fisherman's hat, a summer bonnet, a Santa cape.

Eve watched proudly, smiling. "I've won three ribbons at the fair," she boasted. "I won a purple ribbon for a hobo goose." Eve's expression changed as she recalled it and her voice lowered to confidentiality. "No one else knows this, but I'll tell you. The hobo outfit started out to be a pilgrim suit, but a horrible neighbor kid in a vicious act of meanness glued the suit to my goose. I had to get another goose and store that one for the next Thanksgiving, but the moths got to it and it ended up a hobo outfit. And won the prize. The picture was in the paper, even. So that fixed his wagon, the little brat!"

Emily laughed. The kid was Chigger, she knew, recalling his story of the potato in Leo's exhaust pipe. Gluing clothes on geese was his devious style, although it no doubt happened long before she met him, when he was young enough for goose mischief. All morning she had tried to think of a way to get information about Chigger; now Eve had given her an opening.

"Do they still live there?" she asked casually, holding up a doll-size garden apron. "The Callisters?"

"Emily, dear, please. We never speak that name in this house."

"Yes, I remember. Some big feud with that family. But I thought it was mainly Leo's feud."

"Not at all. They have always been the bane of my existence. Horrid, really. And so hateful." Eve shook her head, eyes closed, as if it were just too much to even think about.

"So they're still there." Emily's tone was playful; she had never thought of the feud as anything but silly, except for that one thing…when Chigger said Leo wanted to shoot his dog. She said mockingly, "I just wondered if I still had to stay away from the neighbors."

Eve wouldn't be teased about such a grave subject. "Yes, you definitely must. How such a wicked brat could ever become sheriff is a disgrace to Bluster

County as far as I'm concerned. He'd relish any made-up reason to arrest a Stark. The man always carries a gun."

"Sheriff?"

Eve, having chosen the two outfits she wanted, closed the drawer and spread the tiny clothes out on the dining-room table, smoothing wrinkles. "That's the only thing I ask of you, dear, just that one thing. We don't mention that name in our home. It has an evil curse on it."

Sheriff, Emily thought. Chigger? Her mind whirled with surprised amusement. How about *that?* The kid with real delinquent tendencies ending up as a lawman! Well, it would definitely make things much easier for her. A sheriff would be easy to find. Emily felt her knees go weak at the thought. Did she really *want* to find him? He wouldn't be...couldn't be...the same. And neither was she. They weren't kids anymore.

And yet, she had to know who he was now, if for no other reason, than to put her teenage dreams away and to stop daydreaming about what might have been. It was better to know. Wasn't it?

Eve handed her a yellow net gown trimmed in sequins. "Want to dress one of the geese?"

"Sure," Emily replied, following behind as the screen door creaked open. "And after that I'm going to drive into Phantom Ridge Village to pick up a few things I need...and anything you might need. I want to see what the town looks like."

They were heading down the front porch steps to the lawn, where the two white geese statues stood like comic sentinels under a gnarled old apple tree, one of the many trees for which Appleyard Farm was named.

"Phantom Ridge hasn't changed much," Eve told her. "But we do have a new county government building, real pretty, built out of the logs of three old log cabins. There are some new little shops in the old building—remember? The brick one? We call it our mall." She slid the blue dress on, and the hat, which was held by elastic, and stood back to take a look at the geese as Emily tied the ribbon of the yellow dress and fluffed the skirt.

"Ah, fine!" Eve grinned, tucking the somber garments over her arm. "Much better! Emily, I feel better than I have in years. And your staying makes it perfect. I'd go into town with you, but I feel like making gingerbread cookies and having some of my friends over for you to meet, for tea, later on. Friends are the mushrooms of life, I've always said. You want to be sure to choose them carefully. My friends have been wonderful to me since Leo died."

Eve backed toward the steps, admiring the party geese. The sun sparkled on the little sequins and a small breeze moved the tiny skirts. "And what the heart chooses for a friend, let no man put asunder."

Eve and her proverbial wisdom, Emily thought with affection. The aunt had a habit of hopelessly misquoting proverbs.

Inside, she ran up the stairs to the pink room to unpack, a chore she had put off for the two hours she'd been here. What was the right outfit to wear to town? A skirt, to look more feminine? No, she wouldn't want Chigger to think she had tried to look special and make a fool of herself discovering he had a wife and three kids. Very casual would be best, but not shorts. Jeans and a crisp blue-checked cotton blouse, tied at the midriff, and white sandals. That ought to be country enough for a country sheriff.

Emily became increasingly giddy; butterflies pitched and dived in her stomach. Of all things, a sheriff . . .

Her hands sweat on the steering wheel as she drove the back country roads into town. For the thousandth time, she wondered how long he had waited for her that night when she never came. Would he be mad about that? "Good grief!" she scolded herself aloud. "It was ten years ago! He probably doesn't even remember me."

It was easy enough to find the sheriff's office in a town of five hundred people. A low building next to the old county office on Main street sported a faded sign over the door that said simply Sheriff. There were no windows, just a screen door standing open. Since the space in front was reserved, she pulled into a parking place directly across the street and then sat, gazing up and down the shaded sidewalks. Was he inside the building? Emily had been rehearsing what she would say to him, but none of the lines had ever sounded right. *Remember me? Remember that one hot summer?* Or, *Say! I know you, don't I? Chigger? Well of all people to run into!* Or, *I was just passing by the sheriff's office and thought I'd drop in . . .*

Emily cringed. Nothing sounded right. She was becoming more tense the longer the delay.

In the rearview mirror she saw a sheriff's vehicle pull up. A man in uniform got out. With trembling fingers she adjusted the mirror, afraid to turn around. The officer was talking to a passerby. She stared at the mirror, thinking it must be horribly distorted. *This* couldn't be him! This guy was thin and baby-faced, with light hair sticking out from his cap. Good Lord, no! It couldn't be!

Feeling confused and a little ill, Emily felt around until she found the door handle and forced herself to get out. She started across the street, jaywalking in the middle of the block, studying the skinny uniformed officer, unable to find anything familiar. Maybe she'd been wrong, assuming Aunt Eve was referring to Chigger.

Emily had reached the middle of the street when another man in uniform pushed open the screen door and walked onto the sidewalk, carrying his hat under his arm. Greeting the others without stopping, he headed toward the sheriff's car.

It felt as if her heart dropped to her stomach, did a twist, and then leaped up to her throat. Emily came to a startled halt. One silent, breathless word formed on her lips. *Chigger!*

His hair was dark and thick, his shoulders broad, his hips narrow in the tightly fitting uniform. And his face . . . too handsome to be real. It was the face she has seen in a thousand dreams. The cute teenage kid who'd kissed her and said he liked her had grown into a man more startlingly good-looking than anything she'd conjured up in her imagination.

A truck stopped four feet from her and honked. The ear-piercing horn brought her back to earth and she realized she was posed like a statue in the middle of Main Street, staring at the local sheriff. When the horn sounded, every person on the street around looked at her.

The sheriff looked up, too. He stood with one hand on the door of the car, and a huge hickory tree along the curb, filtering the sunlight, threw moving shadows gently across his face. He watched curiously as she dashed across the street toward him.

For a reason she couldn't fathom, he reached up and removed his sunglasses, to reveal the blue, blue eyes she remembered so vividly, eyes that were showing no sign of recognition. It took willpower to glance away from those incredible eyes, but she had to check his hands. Strong, tanned hands, one holding his car keys, the other his sunglasses. No ring! That wasn't absolute proof, of course, that he was or wasn't married, or spoken for. A guy who looked like this would have to be.

In the shadow of his eyes, it was easy to lose all sense of time, as though there had been no years between...as though it had been only yesterday when they were sitting on the lakeshore making their secret date. But it wasn't then, it was now, and she was not standing next to a barefoot kid, but a powerfully built man in the uniform of a lawman, with a gun on his belt.

Still, his eyes were the same. They put her strangely at ease, as they had done then. She fashioned what she hoped was her most charming smile and decided humor was the best approach. A joke to ease a tense reunion. "Well, I finally got here," she said. "A little late for our midnight date. I'm awfully sorry I couldn't meet you. Something unavoidable came up."

The blue eyes stared back blankly. "Our date?"

She shrugged and smiled, disappointed that he didn't recognize her on sight. She'd have known *him* anywhere. "Hey, come on, Chigger, I haven't changed that much!"

Recognition crept into his eyes and brought an unfamiliar expression with it. He grinned. "Emily Rose. I'll be damned."

She nodded, smiling. "So, as I said, I'm sorry I wasn't there—"

"Wasn't where?"

She felt her heart sink. He had forgotten! Or was he just covering his hurt pride as men had a tendency to do?

She met his eyes. "On the porch, at midnight . . . to sneak out to your island. Don't you remember?"

A shadow crossed his eyes. It was swift and it disappeared quickly, but she saw it, and wondered what it meant.

"Sure," he said after an awkward pause. "Sure, I do." He shifted from one foot to the other. "So . . . why weren't you there?"

"Because when I got back to the house my mother was ready to leave for Chicago, totally unexpectedly. I had to go." She felt foolish saying it, because she still wasn't convinced that he really remembered. He seemed a little confused over her apology. But he did recognize her.

The man leaned on his car, studying her. "You did disappear in a hurry. I always wondered if you might come back."

"I wanted to, but my horrible uncle Leo . . ."

"Ah, I see!" He was smiling now. "You're here to console your aunt on her recent loss."

"I came to be with her. She didn't need any consoling."

"That's a surprise," he said. "Why not? Didn't she like him, either?"

"No, she didn't. I don't think anybody liked my uncle." Emily's gaze moved from his handsome face, down his body and stopped on the gun hugging his hips. She looked up. "I could hardly believe you were a sheriff, but here you stand, the living proof."

"Did you come looking for the living proof?"

"I did. Does all this mean you've reformed?"

He grinned. "Don't count on it, Emily Rose."

His voice was new, deep and strong and self-assured. Mesmerizing. Funny, she'd never thought of what his voice might sound like when he was a man. Emily wished she had the nerve to blatantly ask what she wanted to know. She drew in her breath. "Chigger—"

"Good Lord." He interrupted her, running his fingers through his dark hair. "Nobody's called me that since I was a kid. My name's Ryan."

"I never knew that." *Ryan.* She let the sound of the name play on her ears and found she liked his real name. "Well . . . Ryan . . . since I can't count on the fact that you've totally reformed, can I ask a favor for old time's sake?"

"I dunno. Try me."

"I want to see your little island. I know I'm dreadfully late, but you did invite me and I still want to go."

Ryan Callister hesitated. When she looked at him that way, with those beautiful eyes, how could he refuse her anything? He'd never been able to before. But he had to now.

He could tell her, he supposed, that he wasn't the guy she made the date with. He could tell her this was the first he knew of it. He could explain that there were two "Chiggers" back then, not one. But it would shock and anger her, and what was the point . . . now? He didn't want to have to stand here and explain about Craig; it was too difficult.

He groped for words that might make sense to her. "I don't go to the island anymore," he said softly. "It's too grown over with wild roses and blackberries. The thorns are four feet thick around the edge."

Emily knew the disappointment showed on her face, though she tried to cover it. It was an excuse, she thought; there had always been rosebushes around the outside of the island. "It's awfully brazen of me to ask," she apologized, embarrassed. "I was looking out at the island this morning, and time sort of stood still, and I was as curious as I was ten years ago. I'm sure your wife wouldn't appreciate my asking."

Ryan was struggling to deal with the odd sensations brought on by seeing her again. Emily Rose had been a very pretty fifteen-year-old, but as a woman, she was a vision of beauty. Her blond hair shone in the sunlight. Her blue eyes were dazzling and seductive. He had been thrown off guard from the moment he saw her, knowing there was something so familiar about the stranger who approached him. Her smile was what he remembered first.

He replied, "I just don't go out there anymore. It's not because I have a wife."

"Do you?" she asked, her eyes fixed on his badge, rather than his face.

"What?"

"Have a wife?"

"I just said I didn't."

"No, you just said that wasn't why you don't go to your island . . ." She laughed, needing the laughter to release the incredible tension that had built up inside her . . . the fear that the kid she fell in love with belonged to someone else now that he was a man. For this fear, she hated herself. She was being absolutely ridiculous. Dreams weren't real. Hell, she hadn't even known his real name all these years. "Never mind," she said with a casual shrug, determined not to show how glad she was he wasn't married. "I wasn't so precocious in the old days, was I?"

"I remember you were pretty good at teasing. But you were shy for a city kid and worried about disobeying orders not to associate with the neighborhood trash."

"You were disobeying the same orders. We were supposed to be enemies."

"Yeah." Ryan paused. "And it's still the same. Nothing ever changes in Bluster County. Even now, if people knew who you were, they'd be gossiping for weeks about my talking to you."

"You can't be serious!" She tried to take this in. "On the other hand, after talking to Aunt Eve, I guess you are serious. I wanted to ask about you and wasn't allowed to say your name in her house."

He nodded, grinning. Eve Stark hated him, and he had no use for her, the way she always backed her husband when he went after dogs and people with that damn beat-up rifle.

"Eve still couldn't deal with my seeing you, I guess," Emily continued. "At least not right now. She might have a cardiac arrest. But the island would be safe . . ."

Ryan shifted on his feet. Damn, she was determined about the island. But he was just as determined not to go over there. He didn't need that kind of pain. And he sure didn't need someone else with him to witness his pain. He'd have to distract her from the idea, which would be pleasant enough. He'd missed Emily Rose for a long time—years—after she disappeared. It was strange standing next to her again...more strange than he liked. He felt oddly vulnerable; it wasn't easy to resist her pleas.

He cleared his throat. "Nah, not the island, Emily. If we were to...say...have dinner together, it'd be more enjoyable. I still know places to hide if the storm of gossip would bother you."

There was delight in Emily's smile. "Do you have a place in mind?"

"A restaurant might be more suitable than hiding behind the barn sharing a purple Popsicle like we did once. A *few* things have changed." He glanced around, feeling eyes on them already. From across the street, faces were peering out from the windows of two shops. "There's a place called Hidden Inn back in the woods outside of Waddleville. What about Thursday night?"

"I'll find some excuse. Tell me where it is and I'll meet you."

"It's not easy to find. I'll pick you up."

"You mean drive up in the driveway? Oh, Lord, no. My aunt is still very involved in your feud."

He shrugged. "You can drive on the road that runs along the dam, park back in the trees on the other side and I'll meet you there."

Before she could respond, the thin uniformed man came rushing out of the office, slamming the screen door hard behind him, heading straight for Ryan. Any observer could see there was some emergency. She took a step back to allow him room.

"What is it, Beebe?" Ryan asked.

"Possum Run, 690, white house on the hill. Got a strange goat in their yard."

Ryan looked disgusted, but made no comment, except to say, "You can have this one." He turned to Emily. "My deputy, Warren Beebe. Warren, this is Emily Rose."

The young man nodded distractedly. He was out of breath. "Gimme the keys to your car. Mine's almost out of gas."

"So get some gas," Ryan suggested.

"That'd take time and delay me."

"If I were you, I'd delay at least a half hour on this one. By that time somebody will have phoned in about a lost goat and the mystery will be solved. And they can go pick it up themselves."

Beebe was red-faced with concern. "But it's eating the *flowers!*"

"They can put a rope on the goat. That's the Aldercouth house. Mrs. Aldercouth is strong enough to rope a bull."

Beebe threw his hands in the air and rushed off, obviously with no intention of waiting half an hour when citizens were counting on him and he had sheriffing to do.

Emily said, "You're one tough lawman, Ryan Callister."

"That's my reputation," he answered.

"And you're on duty and I'm not only keeping you from your work, I'm stirring up curious questions from the passersby. I'm off to do my errands. What time on Thursday?"

"Seven. And Thursday's tomorrow."

And so it was, she realized, thrilled at the prospects of sneaking off to meet him, as before, and as in a thousand daydreams. Never mind the needling feeling that he'd only asked her because she acted so disappointed when he refused to take her to the island. The important thing was, she had a date with him! She started down the sidewalk, swinging her shoulder bag with wild abandon, then stopped at the first shop, pretending to look in the window. She wanted to catch one last glimpse of the handsome Sheriff of Bluster County, and she caught him still watching her. She smiled and he smiled back. He didn't get into the car, heading back to the building instead. She noticed that he walked with a slight limp. He hadn't had a limp ten years ago.

Ryan walked past the dispatcher and sat down at his desk. He'd been off to file the petition for a new stop sign on Foxtail Patch road, but that could wait. He needed a few moments to gather his thoughts. It was a shock seeing her again, just walking up to him as though she'd never left. And looking so good. He hoped she didn't notice how shaken he was. Ten years . . .

Ten years ago Craig had made a date with her, that sneak. Obviously Emily still didn't know he had an identical twin, and by not telling her now, he was guilty of still playing the silly "change identities" game, even after all this time, and even with Craig gone. Like a fool, he had committed himself to the lie. Well, what did it matter if Emily thought he was the one she had the date with? He'd have asked her himself, in time. Craig had just been faster and sneakier. The truth was, both brothers had fallen in love at seventeen, and with the same girl. And she had disappeared without a word.

Ryan was troubled, and he knew exactly why. He had been unwise to make that dinner date, but she was pushing as if she knew damn well he couldn't resist her. But Emily Rose was just a visitor to Phantom Ridge. And she was one story he wasn't going to live over again.

2

THE HOUSE smelled of gingerbread. Aunt Eve, busy at the kitchen counter, didn't look up when Emily came in. She was surrounded by small bowls filled with different colors of frosting and a plate of cookies.

"You've been gone so long I've got a whole gang of gingerbread boys done. I started frosting without you but I knew you'd be devastated if I didn't leave the faces. You always loved to do the faces. Did you have a nice time in town, dear?"

"Real nice." Emily washed her hands at the kitchen sink and picked up a knife dripping with blue frosting. She created happy faces and clothes for three gingerbread boys and ate two others. "I priced paint for the greenhouse," she mentioned, chewing. "The paint is really chipping on the west side. Thought I should get to it first, before the barn."

Eve handed her a jar of decorative candies. "My goodness, Emily, you just got here. I know you've always had excess energy, but take a few days to relax. There's plenty of time to do everything we need to do."

"Okay. I won't get started until we sit down together and plan everything out, figuring what jobs are priorities." She licked frosting from her fingertips.

Eve took out a large round platter and began carefully arranging cookies so they held hands in a circle, saying, "I decided it was too short notice to have my church group over this afternoon, so I just invited Lucille Post, my dearest friend, and Poppy Cassidy, who often stops by on Wednesdays, anyhow. Poppy specializes in gingerbread *girls* and I do the *boys*." She looked up and exclaimed, "My goodness, how cute! You've put little jeans and cowboy boots on yours! You always were so artistic, Emily! Oh dear! The phone. Doesn't it always happen when I have my hands buried in frosting?"

"It's for you, dear." Eve called from the front hall.

It took nearly thirty seconds for Emily to wash frosting and stuck-on bead candies from her fingers and find the telephone in the hallway. When she picked it up, her roommate's voice boomed from the other end.

"I just got in town and heard your message but it made no sense. What's this? You're spending your whole vacation on a *farm?* Isn't that what people do when they have mental breakdowns?"

Emily laughed. "I wish you could see how pretty it is, Jen. There are thousands of trees and a lake—"

"And one little blond fish definitely out of water. What are you doing for entertainment?"

This question brought a smile. Emily was starting to shock herself at how easily she fell into the spirit of country living. "Well, let's see. I dressed Aunt Eve's goose statue in a stunning little party outfit." She glanced in the direction of the kitchen to make sure Aunt Eve was out of hearing range, and lowered her voice. "And I got lots of stares standing on the village sidewalk flirting with the drop-dead gorgeous local sheriff while he was sending his deputy out to investigate a prowler goat—*and* making a date with me. And just now I'm busy putting frosted jeans and boots on gingerbread boys." Listening to her own words, she was vaguely unsure whose voice it was. Could it be she didn't know herself at all?

"Emily! What's happened to you?"

"I dunno, Jen. All I know is, I'm enjoying myself. There's nothing phony here. Everything is so real."

"Dressing statues of geese is real? Gingerbread boys are real?"

She chuckled. "Darn right. It's the spirit of the place. Why not come down when you get a few days off? Give yourself a chance to wind down and relax."

"Me? Hey, I'd rather head for a sunny, sandy beach with a tequila sunrise in my hand and a tanned hunk on either arm. What's this about a gorgeous local sheriff? A *sheriff?*"

"He's a guy I met ten years ago, on my last visit."

"The kid you told me about? He's a sheriff now? And single?"

"And magnificent."

"Oh-oh. A firm, cute butt in a uniform? I know all about the dangers of such. The thing is, Emily, are you sure you want to isolate yourself from the world like this? I was looking forward to our trip to the coast together."

"Be honest. You and Curt were looking forward to introducing me to some of his pals out there."

"Bronzed and beautiful guys who don't have hay in their hair and talk like John Wayne."

"Well, at least out here the great bodies aren't manufactured in health clubs. That's what I mean by real."

"I can't believe this. Something's happened to you."

"Jennifer, calm down. My aunt Eve is the only family I have and we're enjoying spending some time together. I do like being here. You know I've been disenchanted with Chicago anyhow. The congestion and the crime. I'm deciding I like the country."

"Are you still going to England in the fall?"

"If I can get the job I want. I haven't heard yet."

"Well, I'll send your jeans and shirts like you asked, but if you don't get home pretty soon, I just might come down there to check on you."

"Great. Maybe we'll have fresh tomatoes and peas out of the garden by then."

"You sound pretty strange, Emily. Look, I've got a thousand errands to do, so I'd better run, but call me, will you? And don't step in anything in the barnyard."

VERY SOON Emily discovered she also liked Aunt Eve's pals, Lucille and Poppy, who arrived with cake and fruit salad and warm greetings for the niece they'd heard so much about—who had become a teacher and traveled "all over the world."

Emily realized how much her staying at Appleyard Farm meant to her aunt when Eve proposed "a special celebration" and brought out a bottle of sherry from its hiding place in a dark cupboard. None of the others had ever known Eve to take a drink, so explicitly opposed was she to alcohol during her marriage to an alcoholic. But now she was free, and the house itself was free. Tiny stemmed glasses, long hidden on a back shelf of the china cupboard, appeared on a doily-lined silver tray, each one filled with gleaming auburn sherry. Emily found the combination of sherry and gingerbread and fruit salad hard to manage, but she did it, out of politeness, and joined in the talk about recipes, the summer heat and town politics.

Poppy, a woman in her sixties with flaming red hair worn in a bun, sipped at her drink, as she announced, "There's a man named Ronald Coleman running for sheriff next election. The hunters are backing him, to try to get Callister out of office. Coleman is giving out rulers and refrigerator magnets to anybody who'll take one." She laughed. "My stars, he could hand out ten thousand, it won't do him any good."

"Whoever Ronald Coleman is, I'm voting for him," Eve said, serving up dishes of peach ice cream.

Lucille waved her arm in the air. "Oh, Eve, honestly! It isn't a personal issue. We're interested in effective law enforcement, that's the bottom line, and we've got the first honest sheriff we've ever had. One that can't be bribed."

"The toughest sheriff we've ever had," Poppy added, with approval. She turned to Emily. "The hunters want our present sheriff out of office because he absolutely enforces the No Trespassing signs and they can't get away with spraying bullets in every direction during hunting season. He puts them under arrest. Before, it was just a matter of time before some child was shot in his own backyard."

"It wouldn't hurt to find out more about this Ronald Coleman," Eve suggested. "He has an attractive name."

The others disagreed. "He's a hunter's candidate," Lucille said. "If he gets in, we'll all be back to hiding in our houses for the entire month of November. And

November is my favorite month. Emily, have you ever been here in the fall? It's our very best season!"

The conversation turned quickly to the wonders of autumn—clear, Indian summer days and warm apple cider, and pumpkins and various ideas for making pine cone wreaths.

By the time Lucille and Poppy left, Eve had declared they wouldn't even think about supper tonight after the indulgences of the afternoon, and that she was ready for a nap. Emily was glad to be free to walk the meadow and the lakeshore again. She changed into shorts, cleared up the party debris, stacked the dishwasher and hurried outside.

It was the golden time of day when the sun in the west cast a glow over the world and everything was still. Each thicket and dip, each wildflower, each tree and flowering vine, welcomed her back. From the top of a rise she could see the lake on one side and the buildings of Wildwood Farm on the other. There were two houses at Wildwood Farm. The original old farmhouse was a tall, white frame with classic lines and dormers on a third floor and a railed porch across the front. The newer house was a cute one-story log cabin, where the hired man and his wife lived, a couple she had seen only from a distance, for they were "the enemy," too. Did the Tullys still live here, she wondered? The barn was huge and needed paint; she wouldn't want to have that job.

Emily circled down from the hill and made her way along the lakeshore. Frogs, startled by her footsteps, splashed to safety. Dragonflies darted about. Now and then a silver bass would jump up after a bug, sending ripples through the still water. The smell of honey-suckle and wild roses permeated the air.

She came to the fence that crawled down from the woods, through the meadow, and across the narrow elbow of the lake. The barrier between Ryan's world and hers. "Just a flimsy fence," she muttered aloud, re-calling how they used to scoot through fences, scarcely noticing. It was still easy. She parted the wire and climbed through to continue her walk along the shore on Callister land.

What was it about islands that fascinated? They had the same trees and weeds and flowers as every place else. Ryan didn't seem to think there was any reason to bother with this one, yet it had been important to him once. To a boy, maybe it was like a fort, isolated from the adult world. A place to hide.

Suddenly a dog bounded out from behind a cluster of trees, heading straight for her. Emily froze, until she saw the wagging tail. He had come from the direction of the Callister farmhouses, a German shepherd type, black and sable with wolflike markings on his face and clear golden eyes. Probably Ryan's dog. She held out a friendly hand, palm up.

The dog approached cautiously, responding to her voice, finally allowing her hand to touch him. The tail was still wagging.

"Checking out the new neighbor, are you, fella? Nice to meet you. You'll probably find me trespassing a lot around here, which will be our secret. Okay?"

The arrangement seemed fine with the dog. He fell into step alongside her. Before long they were adjacent to the island. She stopped to gaze at it through a cluster of cattails. The ring of pink roses looked soft through the golden glow of light, an effective disguise for the outside wall of wicked thorns.

The bramble Ryan described. He'd seemed so evasive when she mentioned the island, as if the wall were around him instead of it. In fact, there was a stiffness about him the whole time they talked, a kind of hesitancy, as if he really wasn't quite sure what to do about her showing up again. Maybe it was because he was on duty. Tomorrow night they'd be in an atmosphere more conducive to getting acquainted again. Her heart quickened at the thought of it. *Tomorrow night...*

She couldn't keep her eyes off the island. How she had dreamed of going there with him, but maybe she'd built up something wildly ridiculous in her imagination. That name...Pillywiggin. She had learned it was the name of a certain kind of fairy. Once, Ryan had made a big deal about taking her to his island. She wondered why. And why would he refuse to take her now? What was it really like? Thorns or no thorns, there must be a way to get on and see for herself.

The dog stayed with her, sniffing at tree stumps and crawdad nests along the way. She had never been this far before; now the rear of the island was in view. A pretty cove was back there, and where it touched the island was a five-foot stretch of pure white sand, like the tiniest of beaches. *That would be the place to try.* She could swim over and satisfy her curiosity.

Emily made her way to the water's edge where pond grass was growing through clear water. She remembered the snapping turtles, and as quickly recalled Chigger telling her they didn't bother swimmers. Her canvas shoes became heavy as she waded through the pond grass up to her waist, then took off swimming. The dog followed, catching up and paddling beside her all the way across, snorting little snorts as if in conversation.

A few feet out from the island shore, she could touch the cove's sandy bottom. Dripping, her clothes clinging, she made her way to the little beach. The dog was already there, shaking sprays of water in every direction. Huge trees shaded the cove on every side. Clear water gurgled through an inlet at the far end. A few water lilies floated along the edges.

"Breathtaking!" she exclaimed, and turned to the dog, glad for his company. "Well, friend, now comes the challenge of the bramble."

Behind the sandy beach, thorny rose branches grew over each other forming an arch, but underneath the arch was a clearing the dog seemed to know about, because he went through without hesitation. The clearing was an okay size for a dog, but Emily had to drop to her knees and crawl, and even as she did, thorns clawed into her back.

But in moments, she was standing, looking around in awe at a hidden bit of paradise. The center of the island was dappled in sunlight that filtered down through the branches of tall trees. It was a garden of ferns and wildflowers. She found remnants of a path and followed it through a patch of mysterious umbrella plants, and early blooming sumac. It led to a clearing covered in a thick cover of clover. Two homemade swings hung from the branches of an elm tree. Near the swings was a crudely built wooden bench made of old wood scraps that had never been painted. And from a thick branch that reached out over the water hung a rope with big knots tied to the end, obviously a swing-drop for swimming in the cove. It was a boy's hideout, all right.

Another thing was certain; no one had been here for a long time, just as Ryan said. It seemed strangely silent at first, but when she listened, the wind breathed loudly through the bushes, making a sound like whispers, and she had the eerie sensation of being watched. The island felt so strange!

The air felt heavy but as she walked around, there were places where the air, and her body, felt incredibly light. "Maybe it really is enchanted," she said to the dog. But when she looked down, he wasn't there. He had darted off to explore nooks and crannies known only to him. Did Ryan feel the peculiar eeriness, too? Is that why he didn't come over here? Or did he simply have no reason to come, now that he was a busy adult?

The sun had dropped lower, turning the western sky pink. Around the lake the frog chorus began. Delighted, she listened through the chirping and croaking of smaller frogs for the magnificent rowdy chant of the bullfrogs. In the shade an impatient firefly turned on his light. Emily, feeling a shiver, decided it must be the wet clothes. She slid off her T-shirt; there was no one to see. And trying one of the swings, she delighted in the long summer twilight and the island's strange magic.

Presently she heard the sounds of little snorts coming from the cove. The dog was swimming back. Then another noise, a voice. Someone there! She slid off the swing and crouched like a criminal in the high flowers.

It had sounded like Ryan's voice. Carefully Emily made her way to the outer edge and, still kneeling, peeked through the bramble. It was Ryan, all right, on the opposite bank and the dog was with him. No lawman's uniform now; he was wearing faded jeans and a T-shirt that pulled tightly across his broad shoulders. She sucked in her breath, feeling panic. The dog knew she was here! What if he gave her away? That wouldn't do. Better than getting caught that way, she might as well come out with her hands in the air and surrender. That is, after she managed somehow to get her wet T-shirt back on. This was awful. What would he think of her? What was Ryan doing over there, anyway?

It didn't take her long to find out. He was taking off his clothes, getting ready for a swim, and talking to the dog about having already been in the water. "Omigod!" she breathed, one hand over her mouth and her wide eyes fixed on Ryan as he threw aside his shirt and kicked off his boots. He stood up and unbuttoned his jeans. Emily stopped breathing. *I can't!* she screamed inside her head. *I can't just sit here spying!*

But she did. Wild horses wouldn't have dragged her from her hiding place. A bullfrog bellowed so loudly from the nearby reeds, she jumped. The bush rustled. She held her breath. In seconds Ryan was standing naked on the bank and Emily, peering through the branches, was hyperventilating. His perfectly formed body was beautiful to behold. He was a large man, powerfully built and tanned all over. His muscles rippled as he moved toward the water. The spy on the island couldn't look away.

The sound of his splashing echoed through the quiet cove. At least now, she thought, he wouldn't be able to hear her heart pounding from across the water. He swam fast to the opposite bank and back, then stood in the shallow water cavorting with the dog, who seemed to love the game. Why his dog hadn't given her presence away, Emily couldn't imagine, and she waited in fear that still he might. To get caught now would be the ultimate humiliation, far worse than before he undressed. Their friendship would be over before it ever began.

But Ryan didn't come near the island. *Why not?* she wondered; it was such a pretty little place, with the tiny beach and all. Her legs were cramping badly by the time he got out of the water, but how quickly the pain was forgotten as she watched him dry off hurriedly with his T-shirt, pull on his jeans and sit on the bank to put on socks and boots. He left with the damp shirt tossed over one shoulder and the dog at his heels, following a path that led in the direction of his house.

She was safe.

With effort, Emily stood up, straightening her cramped legs. Her skin itched under the wet shorts. Her shoes squished when she walked. There were three itching chigger bites on her arms, and the wet shirt she held had brushed against a plant that left it covered with feathery burrlike seeds. A sudden sensation of someone standing behind her made Emily turn in alarm, but no one was there except fireflies, darting in the deep shadows in every direction so the whole island seemed to be blinking. It was beginning to get dark. A thin mist hung in the air. She'd have to hurry to make the long walk home while it was still light enough to see.

Even if there were time, picking the tiny burrs out of her wet shirt was impossible; they were stuck tight. She struggled into the shirt, crawled out onto the sand again and swam across. Once on the other side, running along the edge of the lake while keeping her eyes on the shadows, Emily remembered a conversation with Chigger years ago. "Snakes come out at night," she'd said, and he had promised to protect her. Hell, if he'd known what had gone on this evening, he'd figure the only thing that needed protection around here was his privacy.

The *squish-squish* of her shoes was too loud as she walked, and every twig she stepped on made her jump, so afraid was Emily that her neighbor might still be out here somewhere. There was enough light left to see the fence. On her right, the lake was still glowing in the fading sunset. Ahead, she could see the white house and barn of Appleyard Farm and the floodlight flicking on. To her relief, the twilight had held off night's blackness.

Two figures were standing under the light; one was obviously little Aunt Eve, the other, a man. *Just swell!* she thought. Company here and she looked like a drowned rat. As she walked up in her soggy shoes and sagging shorts, with her hair hanging around her ears, Emily tugged at the T-shirt that was clinging to her body and tried to act calm. The shirt was so covered with seeds, she looked as if she'd been rolling in weeds.

"What on earth?" Eve asked. "Did the boat capsize?"

Emily forced a laugh. "I didn't have the boat out, Aunt Eve. I took a long walk and got really hot and decided to go for a swim to cool off. Then I realized it was getting dark." She glanced at the stranger, curiously.

"Dark isn't the best time to be swimming in the lake," the man said.

She took a few steps closer to get a better look at him under the floodlight. An attractive man in his sixties, he was slim with thinning salt-and-pepper hair. Apparently he felt he had a right to hand out advice and there was something about the way he'd done it that rubbed her the wrong way. She knew damn good and well dark wasn't the best time to swim in the lake and wanted to tell him so, but she resisted as Eve stepped up to make introductions.

"Emily, this is Ralph Peckham, who lives just down the road. He drove up just now and saw me out in the yard. Ralph, my niece Emily. I was just starting to tell you about her."

"We were worried," Ralph Peckham said accusingly.

Emily looked at her aunt. "Come on, Aunt Eve, you were not."

"No, of course I wasn't. You always were one to wander all around the farm." She turned. "Why would you think I was worried, Ralph?"

He laughed. "Maybe I just assumed it after you told me she was city bred."

Emily glared at him. "I've been around the block and through the woods a few times, Mr. Peckham." Backing away, she turned to her aunt, saying, "I'm going in to change," then sprinted off toward the house.

By the time Emily came downstairs in dry jeans and a loose-fitting man's shirt, Eve and Ralph were having gingerbread boys and iced tea in the living room. Emily helped herself to a cookie and sat down.

Peckham looked at her for a long time before he finally spoke. "Eve has just told me that you're staying all summer."

"And she's going to help me out with the farm," Eve added proudly.

He looked from one woman to the other. "It's time for getting the soybeans planted."

Eve smiled. "We're not going to plant anything except in my vegetable garden. Plowing and planting was something Leo did because he had done it since he was a boy. The last few years, he was busy at the store and hired some fieldwork done. Emily and I are going to lease out two fields and sell some hay, and just enjoy the place. There's plenty to do just maintaining the buildings and the grounds."

The man smiled at Eve and straightened his collar. "This is a damn...'scuse me, ma'am...darn fine property you have here."

"One of the best in the whole county." Eve held out a tray. "Have another cookie, Ralph."

"Don't mind if I do. These are the best cookies I've ever had in my life. A man living alone, well, he just don't get treats as fine as this." He smacked his lips and sat back. "Miss Emily, your aunt has the reputation of being the best cook in Bluster County."

Eve colored to her hairline. "Oh, it's not true," she said with a giggle.

"Yep, it's true. And I never had iced tea this good, neither, with that little touch of lemon." He smiled at his hostess. "I enjoy nice iced tea. I'm not a liquor drinking man, you know."

"I didn't know," Eve replied. "I thought that since you were a friend of Leo's . . ."

He registered shock by opening his mouth wide. "Perish that very thought right here and now! Evil stuff, liquor is. Why, I never touch a drop, never have. Me, I'm for clean livin'. You're looking at a humble, God-fearing man."

This had the desired effect on Eve. She quickly refilled his glass and blushed under the power of his charming smile. Emily had a very different reaction, one of trepidation. Behind his smile were hard, cold eyes.

Ralph turned toward Emily. "Think you're gonna miss the city life this summer? Gonna miss your boyfriend?"

She would not dignify such invasion of her privacy with an answer. Instead she excused herself to go to the kitchen for ice cubes.

Having delayed as long as she could, hoping he might go home, Emily finally returned to the living room in time to hear Ralph saying, "Do you realize what potential you got in this place, Eve? Why, it's pretty enough to be a resort is what it is." He was sitting back, ankle over knee, sipping tea. "Know what I'd do? I'd turn it into a fancy private gun club."

Eve frowned. "What on earth is a gun club?"

"It's a place where people can come to target practice. And do some skeet shooting. The lake is already stocked with bass and catfish and bluegill so members could fish. It'd be like owning a country club." He rubbed his chin, deep in thought. "Yep, that's what I'd do with it, if it was mine."

Emily suddenly realized that Aunt Eve was a rich widow in his eyes. He was playing up to her and, damn it, Eve liked the attention. But why wouldn't she? Probably no man had flattered her in the last three decades.

Ralph glanced at the clock on the mantel. "Oh my goodness, I've overstayed my welcome."

"Not at all!" Eve insisted.

"Well, I'm gonna take my leave." He rose, setting his glass carefully on the cloth napkin Eve had provided. "You're a mighty fine, hostess, Eve. And a mighty fine woman, to boot. I just dropped by to see if you'd be needing any help. The offer is open, anytime." He started for the door. "The country can be a lonely place, Emily girl, but then you won't be alone like I am."

Eve walked out to the front porch and waved as he drove off. She came back inside patting her head and saying, "I must do something better with my hair. Find a more flattering style. Don't you think? And maybe buy myself a new summer dress. I haven't had anything new in years."

Emily's heart went out to her. "Let's go into the city and shop one day soon, then."

"Oh, yes! How wonderful to have each other to do things with, and go places. Really, Emily, dear, I can't remember being happier."

They carried the dishes into the kitchen. Eve wanted to talk about Ralph. "He's a fine man, isn't he? So nice. And so good-looking."

"You say he's a neighbor?"

"He lives in a little house just at the bend of the road, where the old barn is crumbling. The house is hidden by trees in the summer, so you probably haven't seen it. Ralph's new in Phantom Ridge, been here only a year." She raised her hands in the air. "And imagine! All this time I thought he was one of Leo's drinking pals."

Emily wasn't convinced otherwise, but Eve was so happy and so flattered, it would be cruel to throw cold water on her mood.

LATER, she lay in bed feeling a fragrant breeze come in through the open windows, unable to get the picture of Ryan Callister out of her mind. Her first glimpse of him in the well-fitting sheriff's uniform was no less than a thrill, but nothing compared to the sight of his naked body at the edge of the lake. It was enough to keep her tense for hours. His wet skin had glistened in the orange glow of sunset when he climbed out unhurriedly, taking time to stroke the dog. Beginning to fall off to sleep, pulling up excited anticipation of their dinner date tomorrow, she found herself musing on censored thoughts . . . thoughts about his eyes and his voice and the beauty of his magnificent body . . . and the way he played with his dog, like in the old days.

Her thoughts focused on the island. Two swings meant other kids must have played there, so it hadn't been all that exclusive. She thought about the shadows and the fireflies and the odd feeling that came over her there, a sense of not being alone. Maybe it was alive with memories; certainly *something* about it *was* enchanted. Emily was convinced of this because the island was calling her back with a vague feeling of having missed something. Why it was important, Emily couldn't understand. She only knew she had to return.

During the day, when there was no risk of Ryan showing up, she was going back and have another look around. "Tomorrow," she mumbled as dreams of Ryan already began to invade her dreams. "In the morning I'm going back to Pillywiggin..."

3

THE TREES around the cove were old and huge, with lower branches reaching out over the water. Back in their shadows sat a raft Emily hadn't seen last night in the twilight. It was a crude affair, the kind a kid would make. Now old and bleached, it was stuck among reeds, as if it had been there for a very long time. For a moment she considered trying to float it to the island, but there was no way for her to steer.

A swim would feel good anyhow; it was a warm morning. Emily paused on the bank, took off her jogging shoes and set them in the hollow of a tree trunk, and on top of those, her jeans and blouse. She peeled down to a teal one-piece swimsuit and, leaning against the tree, pulled on the canvas shoes still wet from last night. At that moment a rabbit darted out of the brush only a few feet away, followed by Ryan's dog, who was giving chase. When the dog saw her, he decided to forfeit the useless contest, and stopped to greet her like an old friend.

"Hi, guy!" She smiled, stroking his big head. "Want to go swimming with me again?" The wagging tail said yes.

The dog dashed into the water when she waded in, and swam across to the little sand beach. He shook himself off and started through the bramble wall, but something stopped him; he drew away, ears straight up, listening. Alerted, Emily halted, too, wondering what he had heard.

After some tense seconds, the tail began thumping. The dog scrambled forward, under the wild rose branches, leaving his prints on the warm sand. By the time Emily was herself inside the ring of thorny branches, the dog was nowhere in sight. He was off pursuing whatever it was that his keen canine ears had picked up. Some animal, no doubt.

The island was beautiful bathed in morning light. Bees were humming in the blooming clover. Emily breathed deep of the fresh, fragrant air. She chose a different path from yesterday, and walked around slowly, noticing the little things she had missed in the late-afternoon shadows. Like the velvet moss on the sides of trees. And the many-colored toadstools nesting in little shady hollows. Birds were singing all around her, but even in the wonder of a summer morning, the eerie feeling came over her, once again, that she was not alone.

So thick were the trees and shrubs and tall flowers and grasses, it would be difficult to walk on this part of the island if it weren't for the worn paths, and vision was limited. There was a wildness about Pillywiggin, something untamed. The plants and any animals who had somehow found their way here were accustomed to being undisturbed. So she was an intruder, and yet some unknown energy seemed to welcome her. It was confusing. She couldn't help but wonder why Ryan showed no interest in his little island anymore.

This path, like the other, led to the shaded clearing. Emily sat down in one of the swings, shifting so as not to get splinters from the worn seat, and pushed gently, feeling the air fly against her wet swimsuit... sensations of childhood...of times when magic was real. Swinging, she noticed a tree branch bending slightly, although there was no breeze. *Strange.* In the grass to her right, one foxtail in a cluster was moving while the others were perfectly still. She watched curiously. *Fairies maybe?*

The nearby bushes rustled. "Is that you, dog?" she called softly, disconcerted by the soft, strange whispers that seemed to come out of the silence. The rustling stopped but no dog appeared. Where had he gone? *Something* was moving around. A chill moved up her spine. Scanning the area, she saw nothing. It had to be imagination that she felt eyes on her.

From not far away, behind a tangle of honeysuckle, eyes were following her every move. *She has come back to Wildwood looking for me,* he thought. *She is more beautiful than I remember. Emily...*

He wanted to come out of hiding and talk to her, but he couldn't. It would confuse her too much. After all, she didn't know...didn't know about him. It just was too soon. He'd have to work on his approach.

The still figure sat on the grass, mesmerized by the beauty of the woman in the swing, while the dog, circling, investigating scents, ran back to him repeatedly, wagging his tail, threatening to give away the fact that he was here. But he had a gift for calming animals, and before long the shepherd lay down in the grass with a contented sigh, just glad to be with him again.

Emily laughed at herself for watching for more signs of fairies. She left the swing, restless on this summer morning without knowing why. Maybe the sight of Ryan in the cove last night was still affecting her. Maybe the odd feeling of being in an enchanted place. She picked a wild daisy from a cluster growing nearby, and studied the perfect beauty of it, lightly touching it to her cheek. Then, regretful that she had picked a flower she couldn't keep, Emily touched it to her lips, as if in apology, and set it carefully in the grass. Without further hesitation, she hurried back along the little path to the exit on the cove.

When she was gone, Craig Callister picked up the flower gently and touched it to his own lips, just as she had done.

BREAKFAST WAS READY at the house. While they ate, Eve kept coming back to the subject of Ralph Peckham. Ralph had noticed that the yard needed mowing and Eve expected him to be around to do it. This rankled Emily. The mowing was her job. She ate hurriedly without tasting anything, rinsed off her dishes and dashed out to the tractor, which was parked beside the barn. Eve had said the keys were in the ignition.

Uncle Leo's tractor was ten years older, too, and even bigger than she remembered. A large, flat mower was attached to the back, and in front was an iron scoop, which Leo had used for moving fence posts or rocks. She had watched him drive this thing; it shouldn't be too difficult to figure out. Emily climbed on and began to look over the controls. Had the key not been dangling, she wouldn't have found the ignition tucked away at the side of the steering bar. The wormlike append-age by her foot must be the starter, she decided, but when she pushed it, nothing happened. *Neutral to start*, she reasoned, and began to manipulate the gearshift bar, which was an L-shaped affair unlike anything she'd ever seen. She couldn't move it, but on a second try it leveled out as if by itself in what must be neutral.

She was right. The engine coughed when she pushed the starter pedal; it began to roar. Three more tries at the gear arm and the machine shook into action, con-vulsing like a giant cement drill. Emily looked for an accelerator pedal. None to be found. Trying hard to bring to life a mental picture of Uncle Leo driving this thing, something made her push a lever just below the small control panel. The tractor jerked to a start and roared ahead like a scared bull, nearly bucking her off the seat. She released the lever, but the tractor didn't slow down. She was headed straight for the side of the barn. *Where the hell were the brakes?*

There were two pedals down there, but she didn't dare take her eyes off the barn to search the tractor floor closely. When her foot came down on one of the ped-als, the machine veered to the right so fast it nearly threw her off. Luckily, she pulled the wheel with it and, through no fault of her own, missed the barn. How-ever, the enormous mower on the back swung out at the quick turn, and a flowering bush disappeared from sight. The tractor shuddered and bounced. Emily overcorrected. The mower swung out in the opposite direction, leveling another small tree. Cursing, she fought off a vision in her mind of Ralph Peckham walking up about now and laughing his head off, while suggesting it is a man Eve needs around the farm, not a tractor-illiterate female schoolteacher.

The rampaging bull had its own idea what direction it wanted to go. When she pushed the second floor pedal, the tractor swerved left, with no intention of stopping. Emily managed to stay on and fight, while Aunt Eve stood not far away, watching wide-eyed and waving wildly. Emily could see her mouth moving, but it was impossible to hear anything over the deafening roar of the engine. The bush-hog flattened some shrubs at the side of the driveway, took down a small tree and seemed bent on heading for the garden. Emily struggled to get it turned in the direction of the meadow. Out there, in the far meadow, she couldn't destroy anything but the tall weeds while she figured out how to control this beast. Besides, Ralph was likely to materialize at any moment; she wanted to be too far away for him to see her messing up.

The first trick was to keep from bouncing off when she hit a dip or a gully. Only when she was halfway across the field, did she figure out that in this case the shortest way wasn't necessarily the best. She should have looked for a smoother route, around the edge. But that had its dangers, too. The bush-hog attachment could destroy a fence if she got too close.

She was making erratic circles at the top of the meadow, still unable to get control, when she looked up to see Ryan standing a few yards away, waving. He was wearing the brown pants that hugged his hips and a freshly ironed short-sleeved khaki shirt with a badge. No gun, this time.

Emily, seated on the tractor with her hair flying, flushed with embarrassment; he had obviously been watching this comedy act. He was making signals in the air, holding two fingers out, pushing down with his other hand. Telling her to stop, she figured, as if she wouldn't stop if she *could!* She was going around in wide circles, and each time she pushed what she assumed was the brake, it would jerk and buck and start going around in the opposite direction.

Ryan gave up trying to communicate by hand signals and made a run toward her, jumping onto the wide bars of the mower. He grabbed hold of the edge of the seat for balance, got a footing on the floor of the tractor and pushed his boot down hard on both pedals at the same time. The machine shimmied to a halt.

Red-faced, Emily switched off the engine. The air around them, in fact the whole world, seemed utterly still. Which was better, at least, than resounding peals of laughter.

"Looks like you can use some help."

She scowled. "This monster doesn't want to be tamed. I figured my will was stronger than his and that I was a little smarter, but I've been proven wrong."

"There's a brake pedal for each tire. It won't stop unless you push both together."

"I feel like a fool." She stared out over the steering wheel at the deep tire tracks she'd just made. Crop circles.

Ryan braced one foot on the giant tire, the other on the running board. "There are tricks to these machines," he said. "I'll show you."

She could feel heat vibrating from his body as he bent close to show her the controls. It was the closest he had come to her—his arm brushing hers—and the same flash of heat she felt yesterday on the sidewalk came rushing back, along with, to her consternation, the clear vision of his standing naked in the cove. A deep, shaky breath drew in the pleasantly mixed scent of after-shave and the freshly laundered clothes. Perspiration formed on her forehead and the palms of her hands.

"I can't even get the gears to work," she admitted.

"You have to push the lever down hard before you shift." He reached over her, touching her leg. "Like this... From neutral, push up here. Reverse is down and left."

She tried to concentrate while he showed her. It wasn't easy when he was so close.

"Take it real easy on the turns," Ryan said. "This thing has power steering and if you turn too fast, the bush-hog swings too far."

"I can't see where I'm going with that scoop on the front."

"I can take it off for you, but not here," he offered. "You don't want it sitting out here to rust."

"I might take you up on that another time. I'll have to ask Eve if she wants it on for any reason." She looked over at him. "There's something wrong with the speed control lever. It doesn't work."

"It will stay at the speed you stop it," he said. "It doesn't vary in speed like a car. Working fields you want a steady speed." He smiled. "And ease down on those brakes so it won't buck you off. What are you doing riding around on this, anyhow? Out taking a joy-ride?"

"Don't be silly," she said. "I'm trying to mow the grass."

"It might work better if you turned the mower on."

"Huh?" She felt her face getting hotter.

Ryan jumped off the tractor and leaned around the giant tire, pointing out a thin blue stem under the seat with a tiny ball on top. "Here's the lever for the mower gear." He moved it. "You pull that and then adjust the gears back here." He turned a knob. "There. Mower's on. Now you can cut whatever gets in your path instead of just knocking it down. Okay. Try starting it again."

It worked on the first try this time, and with the engine on, there was no chance of further conversation, which was a relief; she could hide in the noise. Ryan waved her on and set off, toward his car, limping, favoring his right leg.

EMILY ARRIVED at their designated meeting place two minutes early that evening. To her surprise, Ryan didn't just pull up and wait for her to jump in. Instead he got out to greet her, walked around the car and opened the door for her. The gesture of respect was refreshing.

"Did you get the tractor to behave?" he asked as he turned back on to the road.

"Thanks to you. I finished mowing part of the meadow and the backyard. But Aunt Eve has fewer bushes and flowers than she used to have."

Ryan smiled. "You need a smaller tractor for the yard, not that big bush-hog. I'll gladly lend you mine, if you can convince your aunt it isn't rigged to explode."

"Maybe without Leo egging her on, Aunt Eve will chill out a little."

"I doubt it. Old attitudes, like old habits, are pretty hard to kick, especially with so much emotion invested over so many years."

"What about your emotions?"

He looked over at her. "Mine? You mean the feud? Hell, Leo's dead and his wife never toted a gun as far as I could tell, so I don't have to duck bullets anymore. I won't pretend I like your aunt, but then I've never known her as anything but the madman's wife. To tell the truth, I'm sick to death of the stupid family feud. When your uncle died, as far as I'm concerned, it ended. I don't have time for such—" He stopped abruptly, censoring an offensive word before it left his lips.

"Such nonsense." Emily finished for him, relieved that he had grown out of his hatred, or at least most of it had died with Uncle Leo.

They drove in silence for a time, with the windows open in the cool of the summer night. Emily studied him, trying not to be obvious, but who could help it? It was hard to believe how perfect his features were, how strong and well formed his hands, on the steering wheel. He was wearing jeans and boots and a white shirt rolled up to the elbows. Emily hadn't known what to wear and had settled for a simple cotton print skirt, small roses on a black background and a light pink blouse trimmed in the matching print. Pale pink, she had always been told, was her best color.

The café was built of logs and decorated with a collection of antique tools and barrels. There were no menus, only Specials, and no music in the background. They sat in a corner booth of a quiet, dimly lit room, eating by candlelight.

"Tell me about you, about your life," Ryan said as he cut his steak.

"I'm a teacher. Elementary grades. I taught in Chicago last year but the year before I taught at an Air Force base outside Madrid, Spain. And before then, I was in Germany."

He looked at her with new curiosity. "A world traveler with a college degree. You've accomplished a lot."

"I consider myself a gypsy, footloose and fancy-free. No ties." She wanted him to know she wasn't attached to any special someone and wished she knew the same about him. "What about you?"

"I'm hardly a gypsy. Lived all my life in one place and have no desire to leave. To quote from old Tully, I've growed roots to the land." He realized from her expression that he hadn't adequately answered her question, because he wasn't telling her anything she didn't already know. "Do you remember the Tullys?"

"Your mother's hired couple? I remember how I avoided them because of the feud. They lived in the enemy camp. Are they still there?"

He nodded. "And always will be. They were all the parents I had after my mother died. Too bad they knew so little about reining in wild teenagers. We . . . I wasn't exactly your model kid."

Emily was moved by the sadness in his voice. "I didn't know your mother died. How old were you?"

"Not quite eighteen." Ryan had talked all he wanted to about the past. Seeing her again and hearing her musical laughter brought back things he didn't want to be reminded of. The arguments with Craig about who was going to see her when. Carefree days in the sunshine. The past was better left where it was—deep in the past. And her being here made forgetting difficult. He picked up the wine bottle and refilled both glasses, saying, "So. Here you are at Phantom Ridge again. It's pretty much the same."

"You aren't."

"I just got bigger and meaner, according to the locals."

She smiled, remembering the comments of Aunt Eve's friends about him. "Are you mean?"

"Yeah, if I have to be, which isn't often. Don't worry, I'll see that it stays peaceful while you're here."

"Then it'll have to be peaceful for the whole summer."

The surprise showed in his eyes. "You're staying all summer?"

"Well, I think so. Most of it, anyhow. I want to help Aunt Eve with the farm."

Ryan blinked. Twice. "A big city girl wilting out here in the country? You'll get bored out of your mind."

"Wilting? If you think that, it's because you don't know me very well. I never get bored. Only bores get bored."

She felt the air around them go heavy with his unexpected skepticism. He was supposed to be happy that she wasn't rushing back home right away. Instead he seemed preoccupied, even a little disturbed. This was a great disappointment. Was he thinking he didn't really know her anymore, and about how little they had in common?

Determined to lighten the mood, Emily said, "I like it here. I'm going to master that vicious tractor and I'm going to find things to plant this summer. I'll learn to make apple butter and pear butter. Maybe I'll even make goose clothes. They're adorable."

"Goose clothes," he repeated incredulously.

"Mmm," she said. "And if anyone comes anywhere near my cute clothes with glue, I'll know who did it." It was easy for her to picture him as a kid sneaking up to the lawn and gluing the pilgrim suit on Aunt Eve's goose. Even now, a tiny, wicked grin was forming on his mouth, evidence that he remembered.

Ryan chuckled. "No one ever proved a thing. I did get into trouble once for stealing a clown suit off a goose and putting it on one of Stark's cats."

"You were a rotten kid."

"No arguing that."

"I wish I'd been here a longer time back then. I'd have been very corruptible and it would've been fun. We could have spent secret time on your island hideaway."

Why did she have to keep bringing up the past, Ryan thought, irritated. It was hard enough just trying to get used to her smile again, and adjusting to her beauty, which was far more stunning now than then. The object of his boyhood crush had walked back into his life, and it wasn't an easy thing to handle. Caught off guard, he was unsure how to feel. Feeling was a complicated emotion, he had learned; a guy took a big chance allowing himself to feel too much.

Being attracted to her as a man to a woman wasn't the same as his youthful attraction. It was more intense, and Ryan was fighting himself over it just as he had done then. It was a tangle of feelings that had caused him pain when she left. And now? He no longer knew this woman who called herself a gypsy. A gypsy never stayed long in one place. She would go away, just as everyone did, one way or another...

"We would have, wouldn't we?" she persisted through his deep silence. "Spent time on Pillywiggin?"

"Yeah. And, you're right, I would have corrupted you if you'd let me. We'd have found a place to hide from quarreling grown-ups." He gazed at her intently. "It's probably a good thing it didn't happen."

Emily was unsure what "it" was and she wasn't going to ask. "You were protective of your secret place when we were kids," she reminded him. "Yesterday you said you didn't go there anymore. I don't understand why, when it's such a mysterious, enchanted sort of place. Not anything like the real world. And probably teeming with fairies."

"You have an impressive memory," he said, wondering just what Craig had told her about the fairies. And she was still the same—with innocence written all over her face, subtly picking at him for not agreeing to take her to the island yesterday. "I can't remember what I said about fairies. It was a long time ago."

"Well, I remember. You said there were fairies, and you also told me you were the only one who went over there, yet somebody else did. A girl, maybe?"

"What are you talking about, Emily?"

"About the two swings."

With a start, she realized she had just given herself away. What did it matter, though? Why would he really care?

"Swings?" The memory flashed through his mind of the two of them—he and Craig—risking their necks climbing out on the tall oak branch to hang the swing ropes. "I thought you hadn't seen the island."

She looked away, then back to him. "I confess. I swam over this morning. I was curious, Ryan. You're not mad, are you?"

He frowned over the question. "Why would I be mad? If you wanted to see it, fine."

That same dark shadow crossed his eyes as he spoke, the shadow she had seen yesterday on the sidewalk when she mentioned their midnight date. It must have something to do with the island.

"It was so lovely on your old swing, Ryan. It was like being a kid again. I guess I'm too sentimental. But no, it was something else, there's something there . . ."

He winced. *My memories are there,* he thought. *And they are mine, and personal.* He wanted to say to her, *Leave them alone, Emily. Leave my past alone!*

Sensing that he was upset about something in their perfectly innocent conversation, Emily sighed, feeling vaguely hurt, and not sure why. Mostly it was disappointment that the man was so different from the boy she had known.

Ryan was staring zombielike at some point in the room, past her head. Emily turned around. Nothing was there but the wall. "Ryan? Is something wrong?"

"I don't . . ." he muttered, then stopped and looked reluctantly back to her.

When he drew into silence again, she pushed it. If there was anything more irritating than moodiness, Emily couldn't think what. "Ryan, I can sit here and look at your eyes and watch your mood getting darker. What's wrong? Is it me?"

He exhaled in a small groan, as if he were in pain, shook his head and lied. "Nothing's wrong. I've got . . . I've got things on my mind."

At that moment, his pager sounded, startling them both. "I'm on call," he said, rising slowly. "Excuse me while I phone in."

His voice sounded odd. Emily had the awful feeling he was relieved by the interruption.

Moments later he was back. "I apologize for this. One of my deputies is at an accident scene and the other can't leave the office. I've got to answer a call. It's out in the direction of home, so I can drop you. Sorry. You didn't even get dessert."

"I don't eat dessert anyway," Emily said, reaching for her bag.

Driving, he drew into himself and was silent.

"Is the call serious?" she asked.

"I suppose it could be. It's a report of suspicious lights in a house where the owners are on vacation." He was driving far past the speed limit, passing cars. "If Beebe weren't so damn worthless, I could have a semblance of a private life."

"Is he the one who can't leave the office?" she asked.

"According to him, his doctor says he'll succumb to his allergies at night when the honeysuckle is in bloom." Ryan's hand tightened on the wheel. "I'm not going to put up with him much longer, even if he was appointed by the mayor, who happens to be his father." Ryan looked over at his passenger. "I didn't expect to have to be called out tonight. Sorry."

In truth, he was more relieved than sorry. The dinner was like a bad dream. Not that he didn't want Emily Rose's company. She fascinated him more than ever, if that were possible. But sitting across the table, looking at the candlelight reflecting in her eyes, made him uncomfortable. She was trying to take up where they'd left off when they were kids still in high school. Too much had happened since then. They weren't kids. She might still be the carefree gypsy, but he was stuck with more to cope with than she had any clue about. It was like being stuck in mud sometimes . . . still dealing with memories and with a hatred for her departed uncle that made bile rise to his throat.

"I understand about your work," she was saying. "It's not as if time is rationed for us, not now. There are lots of tomorrows."

"I'm glad of that," he heard himself reply honestly. Damn, he *was* glad she wasn't leaving right away. "There'll be time to get to know each other."

"Don't we already know each other?" she asked.

"We couldn't." His voice was gentle, but also mysterious enough to make Emily wonder what secrets he was thinking of that she didn't know about.

It was not yet completely dark when Ryan dropped her off at her car. Before she got out he reached over to touch her hand, and his touch felt very hot.

"We'll do this again," he said.

"I'll look forward to it." She didn't delay getting out of his car, because she knew he had to hurry.

SCRATCHING the dog's ears with one hand and holding a can of beer in the other, Ryan sat on the steps of his back porch, looking up at the constellations of the night sky. The mysteries of the sky were no less comprehensible than the mysteries of life, he thought. But life was more uncertain. Planets found paths to follow and proceeded along their certain purpose. The stars remained in their stationary positions, or so it seemed. In reality, even stars were born and died. Nothing ever stayed the same.

Not life. Not himself. Not Emily.

The flirtatious sparkle was still evident in her eyes, but no longer pure innocence. Once she would have followed him wherever he led her, but she was a woman now—educated, self-confident, independent. Her love for adventure hadn't changed, but her world had expanded far beyond his own. She reached for horizons she couldn't yet see. He wanted only to find peace and comfort in the life he already knew.

If comfort was a woman's touch—and Ryan was sure it was—he felt, nevertheless, afraid of Emily. Like a butterfly's touch, hers would be beautiful, but fleeting. And the result wouldn't be comfort at all, but an even deeper sense of his aloneness.

Yet he longed to touch her. He couldn't get her out of his thoughts. She was asking no more than time from him this summer, which was natural enough and fine with him. If he could handle it, if his needs didn't get out of hand. Hell, he didn't even know what his own needs were, except that he deeply longed for something.

Ryan wrestled with his guilt about tonight. The emergency call had turned out to be nothing more than a neighbor with a flashlight outside the house, looking for his dog. A false alarm, like most calls. He could have gone back for Emily, telling her the night was still young. But he had come home instead, thinking she was determined to relive the magic of the past, and that was something he couldn't do.

He had loved her once, but that had nothing to do with now.

Did it?

"Get a grip!" he muttered out loud, scolding himself. Still, their dinner together felt like a failure; he wanted to make it up to her.

FROM HER WINDOW, Emily gazed out at the night. The night was bright with stars. Not since she left Phantom Ridge had she seen so many stars. City skies never looked like this.

"Starlight, star bright, grant the wish I wish tonight . . ." She could think of little besides Ryan's handsome face and his perfect, beautiful body on the shore of the cove. His eyes in sunlight and his eyes in shadow, so different, like his moods.

He had volunteered so little about his life that she couldn't help but wonder what he was leaving out. There was something, though, she felt it intuitively. Something caused the shadows and the sadness in his eyes. He had changed from a carefree kid into a man of mystery.

4

AT A QUARTER TO EIGHT in the morning Emily was in the utility room folding laundry when she heard a knock on the kitchen door. Because of the early hour, she figured it must be Ralph Peckham. The man displayed a kind of eagerness Emily considered suspect.

It was Ralph, all right. Aunt Eve answered with elaborate greetings, saying she was about to sit down on the porch with her second cup of coffee, and wouldn't he join her? There was mention of fresh cinnamon rolls, too. Emily chose to remain in the utility room, busying herself by doing a hand-wash in the laundry tub, where she could hear their conversation through an open window—a conversation that was destined to make her blood run cold.

"Been giving any more thought to my idea about a gun club?" he asked.

"Well, not a lot, really. Emily and I haven't had time to discuss it."

"What's your niece got to do with it? It ain't her farm."

"It will be someday. I'm hoping she'll like it here so much she will decide to stay longer, in which case she and I would be like partners."

There was a silence, during which Emily felt a rush of elation. Aunt Eve would actually want her to stay past the summer. A rather tantalizing thought, now that she was beginning to feel so at home. And then there was Ryan . . . What if she were to take more time out to be here . . . an extra semester, or even a year . . . ?

Ralph was saying, "When it comes to partners, Eve, you'll need to take on someone who knows all about the business. It's not somethin' just anybody can do. It takes a certain kind of experience, not to mention connections."

Emily moved closer to the window. For some moments she heard only the click of a cup onto a saucer and Aunt Eve moving around. Then the sound of her chair scooting up to the table. "Emily is a brilliant young lady. She's a teacher," she said defensively.

"Has she ever fired a gun, do you think? Would she know about targets and distances and setting up a blue rock station, and applying for a liquor license—"

Eve jumped in. "What? I'll have no liquor on my premises! It's the devil's drink, brewed from the root of all evil."

"I was just thinking about gun club members wanting a beer now and then." Ralph defended himself meekly, obviously realizing his mistake. "We could talk about that at a later time."

"There's nothing to talk about."

"Well, the point is, Eve, a gun club would make one hell of a nice business and you've got the perfect setting here. I could make it pay big. I'd know how."

"It's something to think about, I guess." Eve's voice did not share her guest's enthusiasm, however eager she was to please him.

Evidently her lack of enthusiasm wasn't to Ralph's liking because his voice changed, becoming soft and syrupy. "Partnerships can be more than just business, you know. To tell you the Lord's honest truth, Eve, maybe the business is just an excuse for me to get to spend more time with you. I admit I'm a lonely man, but I'm lonely by choice because I've never met the woman I wanted to spend my life with. The Lord's honest truth is, I've never met a woman like you. One with your beauty and kindness of heart. To me you're like an angel, is what you are."

"Ralph, really..." Eve's voice was soft, self-conscious, and filled with joy.

Emily ground her teeth. At that moment she felt it would be a pleasure to kill him. She threw open the door and went blustering into the kitchen like an invading soldier.

"Well, good morning, Ralph," she said loudly, as though it were a surprise to see him there. "You're here early."

"Country people get up real early," he said defensively, responding to the sarcasm in her voice.

Emily poured coffee from the pot on the counter. She took a sip of the steaming black liquid, saying, "Good for country people. I like country people. I like their sense of humor. Like yours. That joke about the gun club idea, for instance."

"Joke?" he said, his scowl so tight it seemed to move his eyes closer together.

Emily forced a smile, glancing only momentarily at Aunt Eve before she drew her gaze back and met the man's cold and calculating eyes. "Well, really, can you think of anything worse than the sound of constant gunfire going on all the time, ruining the wonderful peace of Appleyard Farm?"

"Constant gunfire?" Eve repeated, her voice cracking.

Peckham's jaw clenched, his face reddened. "It'd do no such a thing. This here part around the farmhouse and this shore of the lake would be like a nice resort. Any guns firing would be back in the far meadow." He gestured toward the east, to the meadow that bordered Wildwood.

Oh boy, Emily thought. *If Ryan knew of this plan, he'd be furious!* "Do you think Eve and I don't know how far the sound of gunfire carries?" she asked, no longer trying to hide her disgust. "How dumb do you think we are?"

"Emily, please!" Eve pleaded, horrified at this open hostility. "Ralph is only trying to be helpful."

Trying to help himself to what's yours! Emily wanted to say. She glared at the man, who glared back. He knew she could see through him, knew there was no point in playing his games of deceit with Eve Stark's niece. All this was evident in his hate-filled eyes. *At least we know where we stand,* Emily thought, while her heart fluttered with fear for her aunt. Eve needed protection from this vulture. Thank God she had decided to stay for the summer.

She would stay as long as she had to to protect her aunt, Emily vowed, even if she had to give up the job in England. There would be other jobs, when Eve was safe. Peckham had actually hinted strongly—very strongly—of *marriage.* That was one sure way of getting his greedy hands on Appleyard Farm. And, damn it, Eve looked as if she was on the verge of tears because Emily had offended their kind and helpful neighbor . . . a prospective husband, yet.

Emily knew she'd have to back off and find a more subtle approach to getting her aunt to see the man for what he really was. Ralph knew she'd try, of course, so he'd be pushing his panic button and using all his "charm" to win Eve over, knowing he had a damn good chance because the widow was so vulnerable right now.

"I, for one, hate guns and the sound of them." Emily said argumentatively. Poppy's comments from yesterday's gingerbread boy party came to her mind, the reference to the hunters who didn't like the present sheriff. Would they be the "connections" Ralph was talking about? Just how strong might that group be? Would Ryan be able to prevent this gun club from happening?

Ralph wiped his mouth with the linen napkin Eve had provided and rose from the chair, clearly meaning to punish Eve for the interference of her niece. "Gotta be going," he said. "Thank you, kind lady, for your gracious hospitality."

"Do come back soon," Eve pleaded, flustered.

"I wouldn't be able to stay away for long. I'd miss your pretty smile." He deliberately avoided looking at Emily, as if she were no longer in the room. "Eve, there are things we need to talk about, you and me."

Eve walked out to his truck with him. The rusty red pickup with its sprung door seemed to be parked in their driveway all the time now. She returned smiling radiantly and wringing her hands at the same time. Whatever Ralph had said to her out there had made her glow. Over the sputtering sound of the pickup pulling away, Eve said, "Maybe we could make the gun club idea work. Ralph says there is good money in it and he would be here to run it."

"Don't you want to run your own farm?" Emily asked gently.

"Well, yes, of course. It would just be the gun club business . . ."

"Which the farm would turn into. It isn't as if you need the money, Aunt Eve."

"Maybe it would give my life meaning. Hands not idle gather no moss." Eve began to clear the dishes from the table. "Ralph is concerned about me being alone now and he wants to help."

"What business is he in, anyway?" Emily asked. "What does he do?"

"He's retired. I can't say that he's ever said what he did. He liked this area so he bought the little place by the river with the intention of fixing it up. He's been too busy to do much with it yet. 'Course it's only been less than a year since he came. He helped Leo down at the store."

"So you don't really know anything about him."

"I know he's a kind man with high morals. That's all that matters."

"It's not enough to know about a business partner," Emily said, stacking the dishwasher.

"Oh, honestly, dear, people in the country aren't so suspicious of each other. You'll learn neighbors trust neighbors when you've been here awhile. A friend in need is worth two in the bush."

This was going to be difficult and Emily knew it. "Aunt Eve, you said you loved your farm. How could you even consider turning it into something commercial, with so much noise and strange men wandering all over your property?"

Eve looked worried. "I never thought of it quite like that. Oh dear. Men all around..."

"Lots of men with lots of guns," Emily said.

"Oh dear. When you describe it that way..." Eve continued wringing her hands. "But I don't want to hurt Ralph's feelings for anything. Maybe we'll discuss it some more." She glanced at her reflection in the toaster. "Oh, I do look dreadful this morning. This is one of my oldest blouses. I wish I'd worn something nicer..."

"One day soon we should drive to the city and shop for blouses," Emily said. "We could make a day of it, lunch and all."

Eve smiled broadly. "That would be lovely. Today, after I wash my hair, I'm going to run into the village for groceries. I asked Ralph to dinner and I want to get some apples to make an apple pie. Do you want to go to the market with me?"

"I think I'll go for a walk instead," Emily said, thinking that eating dinner with Ralph Peckham would be a form of torture. How many nights would this be happening?

EMILY MADE HER WAY quickly along the shore and through the fence, heading toward Wildwood. Crossing the meadow would be too obvious to Aunt Eve; this back way concealed her among the trees lining the shore and the thickets beyond. There was a chance she could catch Ryan before he went to work. Ralph Peckham's influence on her aunt threatened not only the future of Appleyard Farm, but the peace of Wildwood as well.

It was a bright, beautiful morning. From beside a dogwood tree, already past its spring bloom, she looked across at the island. Its wreath of wild roses were sparkling with sun-touched dew. Its trees rose high and protectively, forming a lush canopy, closing it in.

Movement caught her eye from the direction of Wildwood. Emily turned swiftly to see Ryan approaching from across the field, his dog at his heels. He was wearing jeans and a pale blue shirt.

The dog ran ahead to meet her. Ryan's limp was even more pronounced than before. He walked as if his leg hurt him.

"I see you two have met," Ryan said when he reached the dogwood tree.

"We have, but I don't know his name."

"Sanders. Usually he isn't so quick to take up with strangers."

She petted the dog, calling him by his name, and remembering Alexander, the dog Ryan had years ago, who looked a good deal like this one. Sanders was probably named after him, she reasoned.

He asked, "Are you headed over to the island again?"

"No. I was looking for you, actually. I came this way so Aunt Eve wouldn't see me heading for your house."

Unexpectedly Ryan reached out for her hand. "Let's walk a little," he said.

Too keenly aware of the warmth of his hand holding hers, Emily couldn't understand Ryan's mixed messages or inconsistent behavior. It seemed as if last night he had avoided touching her. Now there was the warm, sensual feel of his touch as he led her farther from the island. The dog, Sanders, followed, trotting back and forth along the meadow, sniffing the ground.

"I apologize for leaving so soon last night. Is it a problem for you to get away for supper again?"

Emily smiled happily. He seemed much more relaxed in this morning's sunshine. "I can manage it. Aunt Eve would ask questions, so at some point I'll have to tell her who I'm with. Right now things are a little strained at Appleyard . . ."

They crossed over the top of a narrow meadow where horses were grazing. Ahead was a grove of trees, and behind the trees rose the tall old farmhouse where Ryan lived, evidently by himself. To their right the meadow sloped down to the fence that separated Wildwood Farm from Appleyard.

She paused. "Where are we going?"

"I guess we're just out for a morning walk."

"When do you have to be at work?"

"Pretty soon. Knowing what an early riser you are, I was hoping I'd get a chance to see you for a few minutes, long enough to ask you about tonight."

She followed him into the grove, where they sat on an old bench. Their thighs were touching, and heat from his body rippled through to hers. Close enough to smell his after-shave and feel the energy of his body, Emily found herself giddy with sensations of wanting to be closer to him still. Ryan was wearing jogging shoes that had seen better days. Beside hers, his feet looked so large and his legs so husky. She thought of his limp and wondered how impolite it would be to ask about it. Then, as she looked across the meadow—Ryan's meadow—that bordered Ralph's proposed gun club, her mind shot back to her reason for wanting to find him before he left for work.

"What do you know about Ralph Peckham?" she asked.

He shrugged. "Not much. He bought a couple of acres down the road not too long ago. I know him just to speak to. Why?"

"Was he a friend of Leo Stark?"

"I heard he worked for him, at his hardware store. Never patronized the place myself. Is he being a problem or something?"

"I'll say he is. He's been hanging around Appleyard and my aunt."

"Hanging around? He hasn't broken any law, has he?"

Emily touched his knee gently. "Ryan, let me finish. This is serious. He's trying to talk Eve into turning her farm into a gun club, and she's so smitten with him, I'm afraid she might agree."

Now she had his full attention; his body straightened and stiffened. Emily continued. "I'm worried sick about it. When I tried to argue with him, my aunt jumped to his defense." Emily pointed to the meadow just below. "He says the shooting range would be over there, which would make it closer to your house than ours."

"Shooting range?" His voice came as a growl. "Are they nuts?"

She cringed at the intensity of his anger. "Possibly, yes. It's the worst thing I could imagine. I'm going to do all I can to stop it, but I'm afraid Peckham wants Appleyard Farm so much, he plans to ask my aunt to marry him in order to get it. And if that happens, he'll do what he wants with it." She looked up at him. "I figured you wouldn't be a bit happy at the idea of a gun club next door to you, and I wondered if there were any laws to prevent it."

Ryan scowled. "None that I know of, out here in the country. But I'll tell you this, Emily, I won't stand for it. One way or another, I'll put a stop to it."

The force of his threat frightened her. It was what she'd hoped to hear, and yet she hadn't known what Ryan was like when he was angry. She swallowed. "But how can you stop him?"

"I don't know right now. But I will."

"I'll do what I can, too. It would be a disaster for Eve to marry someone who is only after her farm. I haven't trusted that guy from the minute I first saw his eyes. He's evil."

Ryan ground his teeth. "Well, *I* could get pretty evil, if he persists with this idea. The wild animals who live around here would be disturbed by constant gunfire, too, and they've got a small enough place left. Nobody has a right to make that kind of invasion on the peace." He took her hand into the warmth of his. "I'm glad for the advance notice." Then, with a scowl he said, "I wish I didn't have to get to the office, but I do. I'm already late. Beebe will have finished all the doughnuts and had time to get himself into trouble by now. Let's get together tonight. Why don't I cook you supper? I get home around six."

"Okay. I'll sneak over. With a pie."

He didn't make any immediate move to rise from the bench or release her hand. The sunlight highlighted her hair and shone in the blue of her eyes as she sat so close. How could any woman be as beautiful as she was at this moment, without a trace of makeup, with that magical smile? It was unnerving. For some sunlit moments, time stood still. There was no past and no future. Only now.

He was gazing at her reflectively, as he had once very long ago. The memory flashed by so quickly, she couldn't identify it.

"What are you thinking?" she asked.

"Just how...beautiful you are." He moved in so close she felt his breath against her cheek. He released her hand so he could guide her face gently toward his. With no more warning than this, he kissed her tenderly.

Her breath left her as she surrendered to the possessive touch of his lips on hers, a feeling that deepened, and deepened more.

Deepened until something happened in the middle of the kiss that changed it. Neither knew how the shift happened. For her it might have been the quick, heavy beats of his heart against her. For him it might have been the moment her surprise changed to acceptance.

She stared at him dizzily. "I was right. That magical power you have is dangerous."

"I think maybe you're the dangerous one, Emily Rose. Walking into my life as though you'd never left. Causing me to do something as impulsive as ..." He didn't finish the sentence. His lips brushed her forehead gently. He took her hand as he rose, and released it, then, as a way of saying goodbye. She backed toward the deer path that led in the direction of home.

He turned. "What kind of pie?"

"Apple?"

"My favorite." He raised his hand. "See ya."

"See ya," she repeated.

The power of his kiss had rocked her very foundations. The man was a walking dream. Still, Emily couldn't shake the conviction that there was something about Ryan she didn't understand at all.

She halted on the path as she neared the cove, recalling the odd sensations on the island that stood so silently across the shimmering water. Maybe it really *was* enchanted. She smiled to herself, mischievously. The bird songs on the island were calling her back. She heard the call, felt it.

Ryan had said he didn't care if she went there, yet somehow she felt certain he did care. Why he would care was a deeper mystery than his changing moods.

Heck, though, he would never be the wiser if she sneaked back over there later.

THE DIM FIGURE on the island followed her with his eyes. From the shadows of the big trees on Pillywiggin, he could see Emily strolling along the far shore of the cove, on the other side. She stopped several times to look across the water longingly. He had hoped she'd come to the island again this morning, and he was disappointed, but he felt certain if he only waited, she would return. She felt the magic here. Her memories of their days in the sun would be with her, just as they were with him, and memories held a special energy of their own, and would help to entice her back to this hidden place.

She was so beautiful! Her hair shone golden in the sun, and bounced against her shoulders as she walked. Her stride was easy, sensual. Next time he would talk to her. Never mind whether Ryan would like it or not. It would have to be kept secret, like before, but he wasn't going to lose his chance to be with Emily, now that she was back.

5

CLOUDS WERE GATHERING in the sky as Emily crept through the opening in the underbrush. Now in early afternoon, the day was getting darker, threatening rain. It had taken two hours and Aunt Eve's favorite recipe and patient instructions for Emily to create an apple pie, but the result would impress any pastry connoisseur. She had told Eve she wanted it for a friend she met in town, which technically was true.

The island looked and felt different under a layer of low clouds. Emily shivered in her swimsuit even though the air was warm. Water sloshed in her shoes as she strolled under the shade trees, looking around for any sign of fairies. A bird was singing such a strange, persistent song, she shaded her eyes and looked up to find it. A bright red cardinal sat on a tree branch chattering busily. A shadow moved behind a tree, startling her, for there was nothing nearby to explain it. She began to imagine whispers in the low branches and along the high reeds. It was the *feeling* that interested, even spooked her, but she could see nothing, and felt no sense of danger.

She circled around and followed a path back to the swings. Here, in the clearing, one could see better. *Someone was here; she could feel it.* Cautiously she approached one of the swings and sat down. The squeak of the rope against the support was barely audible, yet it sounded much too loud.

A rustle sounded in the trees. "Hey!" a voice called. It sounded far away, but in seconds it came again. "Hey, Emily!"

Ryan's voice!

He stepped into the clearing from behind a cluster of sumacs. Oddly he wasn't in uniform in the middle of the day, and he was carrying a wild daisy.

He held the flower out to her with a smile. She accepted it with a trembling hand, unsure why she should be trembling. To her relief, her body didn't go all hot and bothered as it had the times before when he was close. She started to ask, "What are you doing here?" but he'd only shoot the same question back at her. Instead she muttered a thank-you for the flower and said, "Taking the afternoon off?"

"Just hanging around," he replied. "It's a nice summer day."

"Nice day? It's getting darker by the minute. It's going to rain."

He smiled. "Won't matter. You're wearing your swimsuit."

"You're not."

"Rain doesn't bother me."

He sat down in the swing beside her and began to pump gently, in rhythm with her swing. She noticed he was barefoot.

"Emily Rose," he said in the funny kind of teasing singsong she remembered from the past.

Her heart fluttered at the sound of it. At last they were on the island together. Like in her dreams.

"I never did explain why I didn't meet you that night," she said. "I felt so bad that I couldn't even say goodbye. My mother was hell-bent to leave. She was packed to go by the time I got back to the house. My uncle Leo had made a pass at her and she was furious. She didn't want me in the same house with him for another minute."

"Your uncle Leo was a dangerous man," he said. "He has plenty of sins to answer for, and if you stayed away for so many years because of what he did, that was his worst sin of all."

Swinging, he looked over at her and smiled. In the reflection of gray, mist-filled light, his blue eyes looked silver. "You've grown into a beautiful woman."

"You did a pretty good job of maturing yourself. Funny how sitting here is almost like going back in time and being kids again. You're still the old Chigger. It's a little hard to call you anything else."

"Call me Chigger then."

Two days ago the name had made him laugh. But they weren't on the island then. She conjured up the nerve to say, "I thought about you often."

"I thought about you, too. Little things would remind me of you."

So he hadn't changed so very much, after all. Smiling, she looked down at the flower. "This was thoughtful. I love wild daisies."

"I know. I remember."

She smiled dreamily, resting her eyes on the beauty of him, trying to convince herself this strange meeting—like his kiss earlier—was actually happening.

"What are you doing out here in the middle of the afternoon, anyhow?"

"I'm here because you are."

"So you knew I'd come back."

"I knew."

"The island *is* enchanted, isn't it?" she asked.

"Have no doubt."

"And, of course, there really are fairies?"

He laughed at this, the same easy laugh he had as a boy. "Would I lie about a thing like that?"

She watched his eyes. "I don't know. Would you?"

"Definitely not."

Before she could remind him that the night before he couldn't even remember talking about fairies, he was changing the subject. "There's a log on the other side where the turtles like to sun themselves. Want to see them?"

"But the sun isn't shining now."

"Some are there. I just saw them."

"Okay, lead the way."

"We have to be careful not to scare them."

As she followed for several yards to the water's edge, she found herself watching the easy movements of his feet. "How can you go barefoot through the stickers?"

Her question seemed to take him by surprise. "I'm used to it."

He pointed ahead at a jagged edge on the shore where a tree had fallen into the water. Half a dozen turtles were on the horizontal trunk, lying in the thinnest shaft of sunlight shining through a cloud. Emily was awestruck. They had to be snapping turtles because two were as big around as hubcaps. The man's movements didn't seem to bother them, but when Emily raised her hand ever so slightly, they plopped off the log and into the water in unison, making almost no splash but sending ripples in all directions. It was a fine little show. Both he and Emily laughed.

"Why were they afraid of me and not of you?" she wanted to know.

"Maybe they know you're new around here."

Following the shortest path back to the swings, Emily was still thinking about the fairies. "So, if there are fairies, how do you see them?"

"You have to see them with your heart," he replied, "Love is a certain frequency. I see you in that frequency."

She stopped, because her heart began to beat harder. "You do?"

He nodded. "And you see me in that frequency. It's because we love each other."

Emily, trying to take in the significance of what he'd just said, withdrew into fluttery silence. *Somehow, he knew she loved him, always had. And he was saying he loved her, too. He loved her!* This was so unexpected; she reeled on an edge between fantasy and reality. It must have been this morning's kiss that brought down his defenses. "I can't deny loving you," she said softly.

"Why would you want to? I knew when I saw you again. I could sense it. I missed you for a long time, Emily."

"And I missed you."

Emily expected him to take her in his arms and kiss her as he had done this morning, but not as impulsively. More passionately. Meaningfully.

But he didn't. He didn't even reach out for her hand. She waited in expectant silence while still he made no move to touch her. He merely awarded her his mysterious eyes and his perfect smile.

"Something is bothering you today, isn't it?" he said, throwing her off-balance by changing the subject so quickly.

Flustered, Emily groped for words. Had he said more than he wanted to? Was that what was wrong? She stammered, "I'm more worried than ever about Ralph Peckham after talking with Aunt Eve while we were making pies."

He was silent, waiting for her to continue. "She's falling for Ralph, which means he'll have her completely under his influence. She shook her head despondently. "Honestly, every time I think of that gun club idea of his and what it would be like having guns firing all the time, I get so—"

"Good God!" he blurted, as if this were the first he'd heard of it.

She went on. "I'm trying to work on Eve but I'm afraid she's soon to be a lost cause if he keeps up the courting dance. If she marries him and he has control of Appleyard—"

"That has to be stopped!"

"Believe me, I'll do my best. I hope there's something you can do. Some legal wrangling to do with the rights of neighbors to live in peace."

"Legal or not," he scowled. "I'll try to think of something. Will you work with me?"

"I'll do anything short of murder. He'll ruin her life."

He was already plotting. "Framing him might work. Make your aunt think he's guilty of some heinous crime."

"You actually sound serious!"

"I am serious. All right, strike the heinous."

"You're saying to set him up someway, before he sets her up . . . ? I wouldn't know how . . ."

"We'll work on it."

Thunder sounded overhead at the same moment the clouds burst open. They were surrounded by the spattering sound of rain on leaves. Emily felt the cold against her skin. But her heart was filled with warmth like none she had ever known. She smiled up at him. "You did say it, didn't you? That we love each other? I'm not just . . . dreaming?"

"We love each other," he confirmed in a voice that was like a whisper. "I have loved you for a long, long time."

The rain had begun to pelt her face in great slashes. "This isn't going to let up anytime soon," she said over the noise, blinking up at the sky. "We'd better get home." She started toward the path that led to the opening in the bramble wall, on the shore, then turned when she realized he wasn't behind her.

She could see him through the rain, standing now, watching the sky, with no apparent concern for getting soaked, although once wet through, she supposed, there would be little reason to fight it. She called, "Aren't you coming?"

"Not right now. I'm enjoying this rain."

"But don't you have to get back to work?"

Strangely he took a few steps back, instead of forward. The mist was rising around him. His voice seemed to echo through the rain, "It's okay, Emily." He waved. "See ya."

BY THE TIME she reached home, it was three o'clock. Plenty of time to shower and wash her hair and decide what to wear to dinner. It was hard to think straight. He was in love with her! Funny how he'd seemed almost distant at first, and then *wham*, one kiss and his declaration of love. Even dreams didn't get this good. Ryan had used the raft to get to Pillywiggin, obviously. He might as well have swum; he ended up being just as wet as if he had. He was obviously too much in love to care!

This morning, a kiss! This afternoon, his confession that he loved her. And tonight? Even with heat rippling through her, Emily shivered with wild anticipation. Tonight, spellbound and dazzling—the fulfillment of their love?

"I have always loved him," she whispered to the image in the mirror as she combed her hair. "I have always known..."

THE RAIN did not let up. At six o'clock, when she pulled her small car into the driveway at Wildwood, it was coming down harder than ever, and the sky was very dark. Welcoming lights shone from the windows of the farmhouse. It felt odd, actually being here at this place once forbidden. She had seen Chigger's home only from a distance.

Wearing light blue jeans and a T-shirt embroidered with ivy and roses, Emily lifted her pie carefully from the seat and slid it inside her rain jacket, making a run for the white railed porch that stretched across two sides of the house. Sanders ran out to meet her and walked with her as far as the steps. The door behind the screen stood open. She rang the bell.

"Come on in!" she heard him yell from what seemed a long distance. The screen door squeaked as she opened it, the way a screen door of a country home was supposed to do. It made her feel instantly at home.

"I'll be right down," Ryan called from upstairs. "I'm changing out of my uniform. Make yourself comfortable."

It gave her the chance to look around Ryan's private world. His house was not what she expected. It was furnished in what looked like priceless antiques in classic formal styles. A brick fireplace flanked by wide white columns dominated the living room. Above it was an oversize painting of a woman standing in a field of flowers, carrying a straw hat, the wind blowing her long golden hair.

The ceilings were high with wide wood borders. Paned windows were draped in fabrics of rich colors, a print of deep greens and blues and rose. At once Emily thought of Ryan's mother, whom she had seen from a distance but never met. A pain stabbed her heart with an almost desperate longing to meet her, to be facing her this moment in her home as she welcomed Emily, the young woman to whom her son had just this very day declared his love.

Behind her, Ryan said, "The antiques have been in my mother's family for generations. They were pretty special to her."

"They're beautiful!" Emily turned around. "Oh, I wish I could have known her."

"I wish so, too," he said, then smiled. "Would that mysterious bulge under your raincoat be a pie, by any chance?" He reached out to help her with the coat and she followed him through a smaller parlor, through the dining room and into the kitchen at the back of the house, where he hung her wet jacket on a hook by the door.

It was a welcoming room in tones of wood and brick. One end held an eating nook with windows on three sides and a view of woods and a small pond. She pictured Ryan here as a small boy growing up, and wondered if he knew how beautiful it looked to an outsider. Yes, he knew. She could tell by the way he watched her first impressions.

Will I ever live in this beautiful house? The thought came with such a sudden start, she must have gasped, because she heard Ryan ask, "Is something wrong?"

"Good heavens, no! I'm just admiring your home is all."

He seemed pleased, and said, "If this pie is as good as it looks, it's doomed for a very short life."

She'd been expecting a hug or kiss, which wasn't unreasonable when a guy has just told you three hours ago he loves you. Self-consciously she tried to act as though there were no such expectations on her part, but what about him? Didn't he have expectations? Needing to make conversation, she said, "How do you manage to keep up such a big place?"

"Mrs. Tully keeps it swept and dusted. Normally I don't use much of it except the den and my bedroom. I clean up after myself in the kitchen." He was opening the door of a sideboard. "Looks like we're stuck indoors on this rainy night, Emily. What'll you have to drink? Are you a whiskey drinker? Or gin maybe? Or wine?"

"Do you have tonic to go with the gin?"

"Sure. I'll have a gin and tonic with you."

"Even though you're usually a scotch man, I'll bet."

"How'd you know?" He proceeded to mix their drinks saying, "I'm not much of a cook. I'll just grill us some steaks. Bake some potatoes and toss a salad. I thought it'd be nicer than going out somewhere. What'd you tell your aunt?"

"Eve had invited Ralph Peckham to dinner and I told her I wasn't in the mood to eat with him, which hurt her feelings, I'm afraid, so I had to soften it by saying I was just going out for the evening. I can't talk to her when she's getting ready for Ralph, she's so preoccupied. It tears at my heart to see her."

Ryan looked at her strangely. "I never knew how fond of your aunt you are."

She had to remind herself that he didn't like Aunt Eve. "Let's face it, Ryan, we never really knew each other very well. We still don't, not really."

"That can be changed." He handed her a tall glass.

"I hope so." She smiled, holding up the glass in a silent toast.

They sat by the windows and watched the rain and neither brought up the conversation of the afternoon, on the island. His reluctance to reaffirm his words at least with a kiss bothered Emily, and after an hour had gone by, it felt too awkward for her to ask. Giddy from the emotional overload of trying to absorb the idea of his love frequency, Emily felt the effects of the drink and began to relax. After all, here she was, with the best-looking, sexiest, intriguing guy in the universe, and he loved her and wanted to be alone with her tonight. Chigger was still here—wanting her. What more could she possibly ask?

"I did some checking on Ralph Peckham today," he said. "Made some calls and sent a couple of faxes. Your fears are definitely justified."

Fright quivered through her. "What did you find out?"

"Peckham's previous address was Clydesville, a small town northeast of Indy, so I contacted the Clydesville sheriff and he took it from there. So far what we know is Peckham has been married at least twice, once to a wealthy spinster and once to a well-off widow. As near as we can determine, he went through their money fast before they divorced him. It looks like a pattern. I figure he might have moved down here when his reputation started to get known."

"To find his next victim! Oh, Ryan! This is awful! If you could see how smitten my aunt is—"

He downed his drink thirstily. "The good part is we know about Peckham, and he isn't counting on that. You'll have to find a way to tell your aunt. I'll work on getting some material proof. I've been digging around the courthouse looking for some laws or ordinances we could use to prevent a gun club, but I haven't found any. And even if his gun club fails, it sounds like he'll find some other scheme to use your aunt's land."

They prepared the dinner together, and before long, the atmosphere was lighter; they were laughing and joking the way they had when they were teenagers. It was easier being with Ryan than with any man she had ever known. They were friends.

Ryan lit candles for the table. Outside, it was not quite dark, but the cloudy skies covered most of the light of the sunset. Rain splashes on the windows glistened in the light of the candles. He sat across from her, admiring the smile he had never forgotten and he thought with amazement that they could be friends. No girlfriend from his past could qualify as a real friend, someone to laugh with and talk to, like this. Emily was different. The more he was with her, the more he realized just how different she was from other women. The more he was with her, the more he wanted to be.

They talked over their empty plates, until Ryan mentioned the pie. He got up, made coffee and began to clear the table. Standing at the sink rinsing plates, he bent over suddenly with a groan and grabbed at his right leg.

Emily turned, startled. "What's the matter?"

He didn't answer until he had limped to a chair and sat down. Then finally he muttered, "My leg gives me trouble . . . especially when it rains."

She pulled up a chair and sat down, facing him. "What's wrong with your leg, Ryan? I've noticed you favor it sometimes."

"I favor it all the time," he said, correcting her. "I can't walk anymore without limping."

"Did you get hurt?"

He didn't look up from rubbing his thigh. "I got shot."

She gasped. "*Shot?* You mean some criminal—"

"Your uncle shot me. At close range. My thighbone was shattered and it's been a problem ever since."

"Oh no! Ryan! I didn't know! When? What happened?"

"It's been almost four years ago. Sanders was just a pup then and he wandered across the meadow onto Stark's land. I went after him and caught up with him, but Leo was standing there with his gun saying he was sick of that dog going under the fence and he was going to kill him. I didn't figure he'd fire at me so I jumped in front to save the dog, and damn if he didn't shoot and hit me instead. Claimed it was an accident, so he wasn't charged."

Emily found she was holding her breath. "I never imagined even Uncle Leo was capable of doing such a thing!"

"Your uncle was—" Ryan's jaw clenched, and he didn't finish the sentence. Every word was charged with bitter hatred.

She bit her lip. "It's hurting badly, I can tell. Is there anything I can do? Do you want to lie down?"

"Yeah. Getting weight off it helps. It should be better in a few minutes."

"Do you have pain pills or something?"

"I've got some stuff upstairs that gives me some relief."

"Can I get it for you?"

He exhaled, half moaning. "It's not labeled and I don't think you could find it. I can make it under my own steam. I always do." He struggled to his feet, saying, "The coffee's about ready. Do you mind having it upstairs?"

"Of course not. I'll pour and bring it up. How do you want it?"

"Black. Mugs are in the cabinet on the right."

She watched him leave, fighting down the urge to help him, to let him lean on her. Intuitively she knew he wouldn't want that.

She waited until the percolator stopped sputtering, then poured the coffee, adding a spoonful of sugar to hers.

Fixtures on the stairway cast shards of light along the walls and on a carpet patterned with muted roses. The top landing was a square hall with doors opening in all directions. Two doors were open with the lights on. One was a bathroom. She entered the other, which was lit by a single small lamp on a table beside the bed. Ryan's shoes were on the floor and his jeans were thrown across the foot of the unmade bed, and he was sitting propped on pillows, massaging his thigh.

Finding him in his underwear almost caused Emily to spill the coffee, but she calmed herself with a reminder that she had, after all, seen him in far less than that, on the shore of the cove. He hadn't been so close then, though. Not close enough to reach out and touch. The scar on his right thigh was evident at once. She hadn't seen it from her hiding place that evening in the shadowy light.

"Ah, thanks," he said, looking up as she entered.

She set the mugs on a bed table, under a lamp and picked up the open bottle, which looked like a jelly jar full of water. "What is this stuff, Ryan?"

"Something I get from my vet for the animals. It works better than anything else."

"No kidding! How'd you happen to try it?"

"I read about it. Seems its use isn't approved for humans, but people have known about its benefits for a long time. I decided to give it a try and liked it." He dried his hands on a towel and picked up the steaming mug. With his free hand he patted the bed. "Want to sit down? I didn't plan to lure you to my bedroom tonight, but here you are and I'm not feeling a bit dangerous right now." This last remark came with a smile.

Emily didn't know how to react. What did that mean, he hadn't planned to lure her to his bedroom tonight? They were in love, which made them already lovers, except technically, in the physical sense. Lovers didn't—couldn't—resist experiencing every sensation of their love. His words from the island still sang in her heart, *We love each other...* Dizzy with a desire for him that had been building up inside her for ten years, and had erupted the first moment she saw him as a man, Emily set down the bottle and started to replace the lid with a trembling hand.

He stopped her. "I'm going to rub more on when I've had a few swallows of coffee."

"I'll gladly help," she offered, encouraged, and aching, just to touch him. Ryan only needed to be assured that she was as eager as he for the intimacy that only two people in love can know. He was acting as though he thought he should wait, for her sake, because it was soon. He might be old-fashioned enough to consider it improper to move too fast, which was commendable, Emily supposed, but at this moment, she wasn't interested in propriety.

She poured some of the liquid into the palm of her hand and began to rub it gently over the scar. Touching his warm skin caused the sensations of heat again. The mysterious liquid turned hot on her skin.

"You have a nice touch," he said, watching her hands move over his thigh. His husky voice broke a long silence through which she could hear the thundering of her heart.

She asked softly, "Was Leo deliberately aiming for your leg?"

"I'll never know, but I think so."

She moved her fingertips along the scar. "It was a very bad wound, wasn't it?"

"I spent sixteen days in the hospital. Now my doctor says I need more surgery. I've been putting it off, but I don't think I want to delay it much longer. There's a fair chance of a full recovery."

"But that's good, Ryan. Why have you delayed?"

"The expense, partly, but mainly because I'd be out of work for five or six weeks, and I need somebody competent to leave in charge. I've been working on it."

Emily was aware of the intimacy of her touch. Her eyes moved over him unashamedly, and losing herself to the fuzzy whirls of passion invading her body, she allowed her hands to move to his left thigh as well, moving her fingers, curious and trembling, over his skin.

We love each other. As his words pounded her brain, Emily's hands moved up to his chest, and she caressed him provocatively over his shirt, then under his shirt, pressing suggestive circles over his bare chest. *We love each other.* He had said it because there was no denying the truth. And, as far as she was concerned, there was no denying the passion, either. With her exploring hands, she told him it wasn't right, that she wanted him as much as he wanted her because *we love each other...*

Ryan set down his coffee mug, spilling its contents. He leaned back into the pillows, sighing, and closed his eyes, allowing the touch of her hands to soothe. They did more than soothe, though. Her touch began to heat more than just his thigh; the heat was shooting toward his loins. He unbuttoned his shirt so she could explore further, then urged her gently toward him.

"Emily..."

His voice was as deep velvet as the night. No one had ever spoken her name that way... as if he had said it a thousand times before in secret passages and hidden glades.

As his arms came around her, Emily leaned into the pillows beside him. She felt the rise and fall of his chest as he breathed and the warmth of his body and the strength of his arms. Her head grew lighter, her knees weaker.

"Emily..." he repeated. "You've invaded my every thought since you came back. What are you doing to me?"

"What are you doing to *me?*" she murmured.

"It feels so good to hold you."

"It feels so right," she said.

He cradled her face in his hands and whispered, "You are so beautiful," before he kissed her, in a different way. His heart was in this kiss, and even his soul. She felt herself go limp, and surrendered to her love for him.

The blue of his eyes shone in the shadows of the dimly-lit room, or maybe she was only remembering the blue. The music of the night came in through a partly open window, frogs singing in the lake and the nearby pond and rain splashing gently through the branches. She thought of him standing in the rain, absorbing it, loving it.

"We were a wild team once," he said. "It didn't last long but it was great."

"We were just kids..."

"We were old enough to understand there was something special between us. The world went all dark and sour since those times, but tonight I think I like remembering."

He kissed her again, but it was not the kiss of the boy he had been. Wildness was still there, but so was delicious danger. His fingers wove through her hair so calmly. Like the calm before a storm.

"Your hair is like silk..."

His lips tasted of promise. Promises of wild adventures and heights never climbed. It might be hard to breathe on those high peaks where the nearer one gets to the burning sun, the colder it is... and more beautiful... and more dangerous...

"Is the pain better?" she asked.

"What pain?"

She smiled, running her fingers along his cheek and his neck.

"You make it hard to resist you, Emily."

"Why would you want to?"

"I don't, if you . . . if you don't want me to."

Snuggling closer, listening to his heart, she murmured, "We could wait, but why? When we already know . . ."

He started to respond, but his words were cut off by the touch of her fingers to his lips. "We already know . . ." she repeated in a raspy whisper.

She slid his shirt over his shoulders. Her hand traveled down to the waistband of his shorts, which she teased. Her hand moved inside, touching him, making him moan.

Ryan was rendered helpless by his responses to her gentle seduction. He hadn't expected this.

6

HE REACHED OUT to touch her face. "What is it I see in your eyes?"

"If you don't know, Ryan, how can I tell you? I feel I'm drifting into uncharted waters."

"I won't let you get lost." The promise was as much to himself as to her.

"What if we both get lost?" she asked giddily, trembling as he bent to place his lips on hers again.

"Maybe we already are," he whispered, his breath warm on her mouth. "But you're safe...I'll hold you...don't worry..."

Butterflies were dancing in her stomach, making her too weak to move. She closed her eyes and welcomed the warmth of him against the cool sheets of his bed. His pillow under her head smelled of his after-shave. His breath was fiery against her closed eyelids, so she opened her eyes and looked at him, conveying the wild cravings of her body. He awakened a hunger so strong it frightened her.

"You're trembling," he said.

"It's just emotion."

There was beauty in the way she wanted him...let him know she wanted him, yet he had the feeling she somehow expected more than he was able to give. The way she wanted him caused sensations that were new—

feelings less in his body than in his heart. He knew if he gave in to his passion . . . to *her* passion . . . it might be forever. There would be no going back from here. Ryan wasn't ready to think in terms of forever. Yet Emily was here beside him, leading him to a place of no return, and he was willingly following. More. He was moving into the lead. He couldn't help himself.

"Ryan? Are you afraid of feeling *your* emotions?"

"Maybe," he said.

"I want to set you free," she murmured, unsure why she said it, although it seemed important to say.

He raised himself up on one elbow and unbuttoned her blouse. In seconds his fingers were drawing tingling circles over her breasts. And when his tongue made the same journey she moaned with anticipation.

"Ryan . . ." she whispered. "This feels so easy."

"Mmm," he mumbled, kissing her hungrily, "It's the best way I can think of to get to know each other."

In silence, he leaned over to undo the buttons of her jeans. She wriggled out of them, and when they lay naked in each other's arms, he explored the contours of her body, while she buried her fingers in his thick hair.

Ryan sensed her surrender to him. Somewhere in the midst of their lovemaking, she had ceased to want to lead him, as if she had started this and no longer knew what was expected of her. She might have traveled much of the world, but she was far less experienced than he would have believed. He knew because a kind of shyness overcame her, an uncertainty, or perhaps even a fear of what her own body was doing to her as it soared to new heights of passion.

He rolled over onto his back. "Get to know me, Emily. Touch me. Kiss me . . ." He reached for her trembling hands to guide them.

Her warmth was like flames of a welcoming fire. Like the heat of a home fire welcoming him home from a long journey out of desolate wilderness. There had never been warmth like hers. Never fire. Never a lover like Emily.

When her lips touched his body, he groaned with agonizing pleasure and closed his eyes. She had asked if he could let himself go. His answer was in the heat of her hands and the hunger of her lips.

Then she was kissing his chest and his neck and his lips as she moved up over him. Her hand paused over his heart, feeling the fast, hard beating. No words were needed anymore as she gazed down at him with a look that both thrilled and mystified him. The air, charged with the fervor of their passion, was so hot he had become soaked with perspiration.

She was the heat, the fire igniting the spark of every sensation of pleasure. Sensations of his body with hers, under hers, inside hers. Her face was a blur of pure beauty, her eyes, looking up into his, were moist and dreamy and so alive with desire for him the sparkles of blue were dancing. *Beauty* . . . the sound of the word was the sound of Emily's name. *Beauty* . . . *love* . . . sensations so unfamiliar to Ryan, he felt their intensity in heat that entered his body from hers and wrapped itself around his heart protectively as if to say, *Be warm* . . . *it's all right to be loved* . . . *it's safe to love* . . . *our bodies know* . . .

Her heavy breaths fell into chorus with his, all moments but these, all warmth but this, abandoned. Before Ryan realized that the warmth he felt in his heart had charged his whole body and set his loins on fire, he exploded in wild release.

Emily whispered his name on a great exhaling breath. Her nails dug into the flesh of his shoulder. Her body shuddered.

IN THE STILLNESS afterward, they lay in each other's arms. Emily lovingly caressed his thigh. "Is it still hurting?"

"I don't know," he answered. "My whole body is numb." He pulled her against him and kissed her; his kiss was long and deep and full.

"My body is tingling," she said. "All over. Like I always imagined it would feel to be touched by fairy dust." She sighed happily. "If I could ever see them . . . the fairies . . . it would be now . . . this would be the frequency, all right."

"Frequency?"

"Isn't this feeling what you meant by frequency of love? Of our love, yours and mine? I think something changed when we made love tonight . . . I know I felt vibrations I've never come close to before."

Ryan drew into an unexplained silence.

Feeling his body stiffen, she sensed him pulling away from her even though he didn't move. She asked, "Is anything wrong?"

He didn't move. His thoughts seemed to have gone somewhere else.

"Ryan?" she asked, raising up, sounding concerned.

His head turned toward her. His eyes had gone darker. How different his eyes looked at night than in the daylight, she thought.

"Emily, there's something—"

At that moment the phone rang beside the bed, startling them both. He hesitated, with great irritation, then picked it up.

"Can't Beebe or Jackson take it?" he asked, the exasperation making his voice husky. He glanced toward her as he listened. "Yeah, okay, I'll check it out and call you back."

"I'm not supposed to be on duty tonight," he began in a voice that still didn't seem quite his own. "But the way this job works, I'm always subject to being summoned if there are more so-called emergencies than we've got men to cover. There's a report of a possible prowler in a house less than two miles from here. Nine out of ten of these reports are nothing. I think I can run over there and back in twenty minutes. Would you mind waiting for me, Emily? I want to talk to you."

"I don't mind waiting," she said. "I'll get dressed and make some fresh coffee while you're gone."

He reached for his clothes. "Okay. Coffee to go with the pie. I forgot all about it."

She sat up on the crumpled sheets watching him dress, not in his uniform, but in the clothes he'd just taken off. It startled her a little when he took a gun and holster from a drawer and strapped it on. She thought of the shock of learning he'd been shot, and by her uncle, and she noted that as he moved, he was favoring his right leg more than usual. Or was she only more aware of it now?

How strange, she thought suddenly, that he hadn't limped this afternoon on the island! She thought back to the moments of following him to the turtle log, amazed that he was barefoot in the thick foliage. No, he definitely hadn't been limping then! *Hurts when it rains . . .* he had said. It was raining earlier, too. Surely it couldn't be the enchantment of the island? She would have to ask him about this when he came back.

"If for any reason there's a delay, I'll call you from my car phone," he was saying, adjusting his gun belt.

"But if it really is a prowler—" she began.

"I've been called to this house before, over somebody supposedly walking around the property. It's probably just a raccoon."

She sat staring at the bedroom door, listening to his hurried steps on the stairway getting farther away, realizing that she didn't ever want him to be far away. Lying together in his bed was pure happiness. It was where she belonged, beside him. The feelings of love for him were all but out of control, and she realized she'd never loved anyone but him. And she never would.

And he loved her. She had seen it in his eyes when he made love to her. One couldn't mistake the love in Ryan's eyes, misted in the soft light as his body merged with hers, sealing their love with an intimacy she had never known was possible. Intimacy wasn't merely physical; she knew that now. Intimacy was silent secrets shared by a touch . . . a look . . . a blending of heartbeats and heart dreams.

Even now, her insides still tingled. Her head still spun.

She dressed surrounded by her dream in his bedroom. Had this always been his room? The only sign of a boy here was a worn stuffed teddy bear on one of the dresser tops. Emily touched the bear, smiling. The tough sheriff had been a child once, and he hadn't parted with his bear. Walnut and cherry antiques lined the walls of his room—a massive dresser with carved feet, an overstuffed chair in a blue print that matched the blue of the curtains. Carved headboards and matching tables on either side of the twin beds. There were books and magazines piled on the tables and on the dresser, but no dirty clothes around, very little clutter.

The whole house must be furnished in these lovely pieces, she thought, tying her shoes. Her curiosity demanded a peek into the other bedrooms.

Emily slid into the hallway, and opened one of the closed bedroom doors. The scent of dust permeated the room; apparently Mrs. Tully didn't bother cleaning in here. She switched on the light. It was a lovely room with rose curtains and a rose patterned bedspread under a lacy canopy. The bed was so high, two steps covered in tapestry sat beside it. She knew immediately it was his mother's room. He must have left this room just as it was.

She took in the ambience, the beauty. The focal point of the room were leaded glass bookcases against one wall framing an antique writing desk. In the chair sat another teddy bear, as if it were keeping some kind of vigil. Except for being black instead of brown, the bear was exactly like the one in Ryan's room, and just as worn. Odd that he'd have two identical bears . . .

Her eyes scanned the room, taking in its elegant details. On an ornate cherry dresser was a photo in a silver frame, which appeared to be Ryan standing beside . . . himself! Puzzled, she picked it up. He was a teenager, about the age she'd first met him, smiling, with one arm around the shoulders of his exact double. The photo began to tremble in her hands. Emily stared down at it for a long time. There was no mistaking what she saw—the two boys had the same face, the same smile. *They were identical twins.*

But that simply couldn't be. Her troubled eyes glanced away from the illusion, only to come to rest on a smaller photo on the writing desk of two identical boys about age nine, alongside still another of two toddlers with their mother. She moved to the desk and picked the picture of the two smiling baby boys held on the arms of their mother's chair, dressed in identical coveralls and red shirts. On the back was written in careful script with a heavy marker, *Craig and Ryan, age 27 months.*

A gray cloud of mystery rose from the dust of the room and engulfed her, and the dust caused her to choke. She began to feel ill. What she was seeing was impossible. How could Ryan have a twin? But the proof was in her hands; he did . . . and his twin's name was Craig. But where was Craig? Why had she never seen him?

There were memories of him here, in their mother's empty room. On a small drop-leaf table near the window were two thick books that looked like photo albums. Tensing like an unwelcome intruder, Emily sat down on a chair beside the table and opened one of the books. Family pictures. Photos of two identical babies. Their father was in the early pictures, the father whom Ryan had mentioned only once long ago, saying his parents had divorced.

Numbly Emily leafed through this family record of two boys growing up. Only a few pictures were of only one child, and these were always labeled either *Ryan* or *Craig*.

She reached the pages of their teen years. Then their high school yearbook pictures, the familiar grin she knew belonged to ... to Chigger. Reeling, she whispered into the hollow silence of the room, *"Where was Craig?"* Why didn't I meet him? Why has Ryan never mentioned him? Never even mentioned ...

On the last pages were several photos of boys becoming men. One of the brothers working on the cabin bare-chested, smiling, holding beers. And another that looked as if had been taken at a local fair ... Ryan in his sheriff's uniform and his twin standing beside him. This one was very recent. Except for the uniform, she couldn't possibly tell the two apart. Her heart was pounding by the time she closed the book. Something was horribly, terribly wrong. One didn't hide the fact that he had an identical twin. What possible reason could Ryan have?

She turned off the lamp and left the sad room of dust and memories, no longer hearing the squeaking of the old floors under her feet. When she'd made her way down the steps and into the warmth and cheerfulness of the kitchen, it looked the same as before, but nothing felt the same.

The feeling she'd had yesterday and today about Ryan keeping something from her...now she knew what it was. The mystery was *why?* Moving around the kitchen, Emily started through the familiar motions of making coffee...smelling coffee grounds, hearing the sound of running water, yet her senses were elsewhere, her mind caught in quicksand and sinking faster into stark reality than she wanted to. That summer long ago—why hadn't she met both brothers then?

Or had she?

Her alert, now wary, brain began to pull out recorded thoughts and memories fast and furiously, like a kaleidoscope of shapes and colors all rushing at her at once, striking so hard she wished she could dodge the hits.

He didn't limp on the island! And now that she thought about it, he seemed confused by what she meant when she repeated his explanation of love frequency. And the difference in his eyes? *The difference in his eyes!* Emily felt a freezing chill move through her spine and stop at the level of her heart. *Oh my God...*

Their voices were not exactly the same, now that she really thought about it. On the island he sounded... different, lighthearted, more like the boy she had once known. She still heard his voice, declaring his love for her, etching those words on her heart. But, here, tonight, was that other voice, darker and deeper, which had never said anything about love...the voice that belonged to the man she had just brazenly fondled to distraction. Ensnared in her erotic lust.

Her face burned with the flames of anger and shame. It hadn't been Ryan on the island. It couldn't have been!

Emily slammed her fist so hard on the table, it hurt, but not enough to distract her from the horror unfolding before her. On the island...the island...it had been Craig who said he loved her! And she had come to Ryan's bed ...

Tears welled to the surface and spilled down her face. What a fool she'd made of herself. What a fool they had made of her! The heat shot out from her head to her chest and she began to ache all over. What was the purpose of this deception? Some stupid game of theirs? No other explanation presented itself no matter how desperately she wanted to believe that Ryan couldn't sink so low. The guy on the island wasn't Ryan.

Had they tricked her ten years ago, too? The memories ran like an animated tape through her mind. Ryan's puzzled look when she mentioned their midnight date. Maybe he didn't remember because he wasn't even there!

Oh God. Who was Chigger? For that matter, who was Ryan?

Emily felt as if she had just been tossed up on a rocky shore by a killer wave and left bleeding and dying and not knowing why. Only in a nightmare could all dreams dissolve and disappear in a few fractured moments of time.

She didn't hear his car enter the driveway before the slam of the door. He came in the back door, into the kitchen, and saw her sitting at the table, her head bent into her arms. She raised her head to face him, her cheeks streaked with tears. A sob caught the first breath she took.

He rushed toward her. "Emily! What's the matter?"

She stared at him through the silver shine of tears. Silence filled the room.

Ryan sat down next to her and touched her arm, and she flinched. She pulled her hand away.

"Emily? For God's sake, tell me."

She wiped the tears with the back of her hand as she forced her fear into stumbling, audible words. "Which one are you?"

"What?"

She looked, finally, into Ryan's sky blue eyes and repeated, "Which one are you?"

He drew back, and she finally broke the silence with an intake of breath that was barely under control. "Why haven't you ever told me about your twin brother?"

The shadow that crossed his eyes had no description but pain. If she had expected deceit or laughter or anger or capitulation, all she could see in the shadow was pain. It unnerved her, took her back into the horror of the mystery.

Ryan swallowed. His voice came out like a raspy whisper. "I intended to. Actually I intended to tell you tonight. But how did you—?"

"The photographs. I suppose I shouldn't have been nosy. I was just going to peek at what the other rooms look like because every room in this house is so pretty." She choked on a sob. "I just . . . I saw the pictures of the two of you."

He started to touch her hand again and stopped himself. "But you were crying. I can understand why it might have been a shock to see pictures of me with my brother . . . but why would it . . . make you cry?"

"Why?" Her breaths were trembling. "You can ask why, after humiliating me like you have?" She stared at him. "You tricked me! You made a fool of me!"

"We did," he confessed sadly. "But it was—"

"From all the way back when I first met you," she said, interrupting him. "Did you exchange identities?"

He nodded. "It was a rotten thing to do. We were rotten kids, and I'm sorry for it now."

"But you're still doing it!"

He fell strangely silent, and it frightened her.

"How could you?" she asked. "And where the hell *is* he...?" Her sobs threatened to get out of control again. The sobs were embarrassing her, making it worse. She clenched her teeth and breathed deeply and forced herself with all the willpower she could muster to stop the sniveling and act like a woman instead of a wounded girl. "Is he here? In this house, refusing to come out or something?"

The bewildering pain lingered in Ryan's eyes. She couldn't look at him, and turned away, pleading, "Where the hell *is* he, Ryan?"

"My brother is dead, Emily."

"Wh...what?" She looked back. "I don't...believe you."

"Craig died over a year ago."

"But that's impossible! I...saw him! On the island. I know it wasn't you..." Anger began to boil inside her. She saw him as a stranger, someone so deceitful as to be dangerous. "You're lying!"

A blinding pain pierced Ryan's temples, a pain so severe, he suffered a momentary blackout. He heard his own voice trembling as if it were the voice of someone he didn't know. "Saw him? What are you saying?"

"Mainly I'm saying I don't like being made a fool of!" She struggled to contain her rage. She raised her arms into the air. "Such an *elaborate* hoax! I just can't fathom why!" She met his eyes, all the more confused by the incredible pain she saw in them.

She couldn't take another second of looking at him, after the love they had shared tonight, after the joy she had felt, believing he loved her. If he would go so far as to say his twin was dead, when she had just seen him on the island this afternoon—just how far *would* they have taken this hoax?

After the joy of last hour, Emily was stricken with the torment of her heart breaking, and his witnessing her distress was just making it worse. Later she'd confront him and demand some explanation . . . later, when she could think...later, when she wasn't hurting so much. She rose, holding her head high. "I can't stand any more lies, Ryan. I'm leaving."

He shook his head, as if trying to pull himself out of a fog. "Emily, please . . ."

She winced from the sincere ring of his plea. "I don't want to talk. I really had thought—" She couldn't, wouldn't finish the sentence, maybe not ever. She really had thought he loved her. And it hadn't even been Ryan who'd said it . . .

"Your eyes are vivid blue," she said softly, as if to herself and not to him. "His eyes are silver. Your voice is deep and gruff and his is...his is light, happy. He goes barefoot and doesn't limp. I'm not fooled, anymore, Ryan. I know there are two of you."

Blindly she made her way out the back door and into the driveway, and got into her car. He didn't try to stop her. She crept the half mile home, grateful to see the lights out in Eve's bedroom. It would be easy to sneak into the house in the dark, especially now that the rain had stopped. She needed darkness. Darkness could help absorb pain, though maybe not this time. The agony that caught her in its grip tonight was too deep to be absorbed.

By tomorrow, though, she vowed, she would find the strength to confront them. Both of them!

Getting undressed, she could still feel Ryan against her body. She could smell his after-shave on her skin. And feel the sensations of his love. It was Ryan, wasn't it? Yes. Ryan was scarred by bullets from Leo Stark's gun.

Where was Craig when he wasn't on the island? And why would he hang out there? Just there?

The more the thoughts churned and mixed together in her head, the more Emily realized something was even more wrong than she had originally, in her hysterics, imagined. Why the awful pain in Ryan's eyes? And why ever would he want her to think his brother was dead?

Every anticipated answer was horrible because it smacked of deceit and trickery. Overcome with anger, Emily swore she wouldn't be deceived anymore. She wanted the truth and she was going to get it. From both damn Chiggers!

RYAN TURNED out the kitchen light and sat staring into the darkness toward the lake and the island. The storm had blown over and clouds were timidly parting near the moon, allowing scallops of gold to shine through. His head was swimming.

Was Emily delusional?

Tonight, for the first time since Craig had died, he felt the first awakenings of his own feelings. Making love to her, he knew joy beyond imagining, because in Emily's eyes he saw pure and honest love . . . love for him, and his heart had begun to dance in rhythms he'd never felt before.

And then there was her pain. How could she have imagined she had seen, talked to Craig? He had to forcibly remind himself that his brother was no longer alive, no longer here, with his laughter filling the house, and his mischief still at work. The grief of losing him was still too new to absorb. Moisture blurred his eyes as if it were misty rain.

Out there, over the island, a nearly full moon was showing between whirls of night-walking clouds. Ryan rose, his heart beating hard against his aching chest. The cold, bright moon threw out a path of light to see by. He had to follow it. He had to know.

7

HE WAS AT HOME in darkness. He knew by heart the patterns of stars, and his night vision was excellent. By now the sky was pierced with tiny barbs of light. From the edge of the cove, Ryan gazed at the moon path reflected on the dark surface of the water. Carrying a long, lightweight rope, he made his way to the edge of the water where the old raft rested in the reeds. He found a fallen tree branch and stepped onto the worn, flat surface. Sanders jumped on with him, and Ryan shoved off, guiding the raft along the shallow water with the branch until he was close enough to the island to toss the rope into the bramble. After a few tries, it caught, and he pulled them in to the sand beach.

The dog, tail wagging, leaped off and scrambled through the thicket and into the shadows, as if he had a destination in mind and knew why Ryan had come. As soon as Ryan ducked through the overhang of branches, he felt the awful rush of sadness that had hung around him since the day his brother died. Just seventeen months ago, the accident seemed like yesterday; the pain was still raw. Nothing in his life had been the same since. Determination to get Leo Stark for murdering his brother had consumed him. He knew Stark had forced Craig over that weakened bridge at gunpoint, but Ryan could never prove it. His obsession for revenge, added to the grief over the loss of his brother, had cost his peace of mind.

The shadows in the moonlight were familiar; as kids the twins had come here often when the moon was bright. Even, sometimes, on nights like this when the remains of a summer rain dripped from the leaves, and drenched grass clung to his boots. Frogs were beginning to sing again, after the refreshing storm, and a few crickets chirped in their dry hiding places. A thousand memories invaded Ryan's mind, and the memories hurt. Maybe he should have had the guts to come sooner; he just hadn't been able to make himself do it. Now he knew why. The island felt strangely alive and filled with whispers, as though Craig were here waiting for him.

Aching with the agony of deep loss, Ryan followed the old path, grown over, but still visible, his keen eyes adjusting well to the dim light. The swings appeared in silhouette, still and silent. Bewildered and confused over Emily's hysterics, and not knowing what else to do, he sat down on one of the wet swings and pushed it absently into motion.

"That's my swing." Craig's voice echoed from the shadows.

Startled, Ryan looked up, almost expecting to see his brother standing under the towering cottonwood, where they once made roads for their toy trucks. Craig wasn't there. Yet his voice had been so clear. It felt like, sounded like, the mental telepathy the twins had cultivated and practiced all their lives.

"That *is* my swing," the voice repeated. "And Emily is my girl."

Ryan knew he wasn't dreaming. Craig's message was coming through loud and clear. By how? And why here? Although his hands trembled as he held the rain-soaked ropes of the swing, Ryan began to feel an extraordinary sense of calm. Craig was here, as always. He felt his presence, and it felt so strangely right. Sanders was jumping around by the tree, behaving as he did when he was greeting someone. He knew Craig was here.

In response to Ryan's silence, Craig said, "You came over to find me, so why are you so surprised?"

"Because both of us always swore we didn't believe in ghosts."

Craig's laughter echoed softly. "So we were wrong. Live and learn. Or die and learn, as the case may be."

Ryan couldn't understand his feeling of calm or why it felt so natural hearing Craig's voice and his laugh again, unchanged. "I don't get it, Craig! What's going on?" He swallowed hard and felt a stab at his heart. "Where the hell *are* you?"

"Not hell. I'm just behind a veil in the next dimension. It isn't far, it just seems far that way when we're in human form." Craig laughed. "You'll see for yourself someday. It's good, though, it's fine."

The other swing began to move, as if Craig were sitting there, swinging, as he had a thousand times before. He was that close. Ryan began to fidget, wanting answers. One of the worst things he'd ever had to go through was not being able to talk to his brother after a lifetime of closeness. Now he could, and it felt good and not good at the same time. He said, "It's been tough having you gone." His mind whirled and gnarled with dozens of disturbing questions he had ached to have answers for. "I tried my damnedest to arrest Leo Stark, to prove he was responsible for your...death. There were no witnesses. Right up until Stark died, I was still trying—"

"Hey! Forget all that. It wasn't Leo's fault. I wish it were, but the truth is, I was the one to blame."

Shocked, Ryan stared at the shine of moonlight where he imagined his brother to be. "You were? How? What the devil happened?"

"It doesn't matter, don't you see?"

"What do you mean, it doesn't matter?" Ryan was astounded. "I figured Leo had a gun on you and deliberately forced you off his property in that direction, and that he knew the bridge was dangerous."

"Nope, you're wrong. If I hadn't been so damn furious and in such a rush, I wouldn't have gone that way. He didn't stop me, but then, I don't think he even knew which way I was going. I have only myself to blame." He was as calm as if they were discussing the weather. "I hit my head and knocked myself unconscious, otherwise I probably could have got out of the truck. Stark heard the noise and called for help. He didn't delay like you thought. So let it go, Ryan. You've got to release all that crap and get on with your life. You're twenty-seven now. Why the hell didn't you marry Jenny?"

He shrugged. "Hell, I dunno. I lost all interest in everything, including getting married. After you... died, I just wanted to be alone. Besides, I didn't want Jenny."

"Well, you're alone. Do you like it?"

Ryan swallowed. "I don't know." A rush of cold, then deep warmth came over him. He hadn't been alone earlier tonight.

"Emily Rose is back," Craig said, as if he had read his mind. "Might it be her you want?"

Remembering Emily's words, which he had momentarily forgotten in the emotional storm of reuniting with his brother, caused a shiver at the base of Ryan's spine.

"I saw her," Craig said. "She's even more beautiful than before. She was the only girl I ever really loved, you know. You didn't answer my question, Ry. Do you want her, too?"

Ryan sat speechless, unable to believe what he was hearing.

"I did once," he stammered. "I still do. I don't know . . ."

Craig cursed. "It's not fair. You being alive, you've got a better chance."

You've got that right! Ryan thought. Craig was a ghost; he didn't have a hope in hell, let's face it.

Craig continued. "It's me she loves, I know that, but I'm at a disadvantage, of course. She's mine, though. Get that straight."

Ryan wondered if he might be dreaming this. He was talking to a *spirit*, albeit one he had known since birth. "I don't get you," he said finally. "You're saying Emily was your true love? A girl we knew only for a few weeks?"

"That's right. You felt the same. Don't deny it. And you never fell in love again, either, not that way. I think it's why you drove Jenny away."

Ryan scowled. He should have known better than to think he had any secrets from his twin. Something was wrong with this, he thought numbly, but his brain couldn't focus on exactly what because he was working so hard at keeping his emotions in control. It was amazing to him how feelings of before were unchanged. Although he couldn't see him, Craig was just the same. One part of Ryan was awed and thankful to be able to communicate with his brother again. Another part wasn't so sure. He had suffered like hell after Craig's death and worked hard for closure so he could get on with living; now maybe the closure he needed would never be possible.

A small cloud floated in front of the moon. The sudden darkness disturbed him, brought on a sense of helplessness. He desperately wanted his brother back, but not like this! He got out of the swing and stood up. "I'm almost too dazed to think," he said. "Somehow, I had this feeling you weren't gone forever, and yet you are..." He took a step in the direction of the raft. "This is tough, Craig."

"Yeah, I know." The voice was beginning to fade. "But I had to get in touch with you. You were ruining your life trying to avenge my death, and you didn't have the facts right. I had to release you from that anger."

As Ryan listened, the words were fading in and out. He realized the force of Craig's words, though. The voice was like an echo now, becoming weaker. "I've learned a couple things, being over here. This thing about revenge. All it does is hurt the one who wants it. Believe me, Leo has to answer for what he did, over here. We all do. So that's what I wanted to tell you. I wasn't murdered. I was killed because of my own misjudgment. Leo the madman didn't do it."

As the cloud moved from over the moon, the island became shadowy white and still. Ryan no longer felt the presence so near. He could hear only the voices of night—singing frogs and the eerie cry of an owl across the cove. Loneliness enveloped him again, but a weight had been lifted off his shoulders.

"Craig, wait," he hollered. "I don't get it! Why can't I see you, and she can?"

The voice was patient. "You could see me if I tried, but I have to expend a hell of a lot of willpower and energy to actually materialize and I don't have to do it to communicate with you. With you it isn't so different from before."

Ryan was astounded. "You mean you can just pop up—"

"It only works here on old Pillywiggin. At least so far. I've been trying to expand the materializing skills elsewhere but no luck so far. It's difficult. Here the vibration is exactly right."

"So your love for this girl we once knew as kids was what gave you the power to do this? Your love for your brother wasn't strong enough?"

There was a rustle in the wet leaves as if the ghost were moving closer. Ryan thought a shadow glanced over a patch of spring daisies just in front of him.

"Hey, come on!" Craig answered. "Stronger isn't what works. It was Emily's openness and acceptance and her innocence. Your bitterness over my accident and blaming Stark was blocking the energy. I couldn't get through the density of your anger."

"But you did it last night. And you're doing it now. Because of her?"

"No, damn it. Because you wouldn't come over to our island. Besides which, my love for her isn't a one-way force. Her love was helping to pull me back."

The remark rankled Ryan. It sounded like the old Craig, the one who never stopped competing. "How can you say she loves you when she thinks you're me?"

"Wrong. She thinks you're *me*."

"Blast it, how could she know the difference, Craig? She has no idea she was talking to a ghost. It isn't fair to her."

"That's true, and if you tell her, she'll think you're nuts."

Ryan swallowed. "I don't want to play this stupid game. It was bad enough that we tricked her when we were kids. What the hell did you say to her, anyhow? Did you say you were in love with her?"

"Sure. Would a spirit lie? I said we were in love with each other, and she agreed. She's in love with me, that's how it is."

A strange anger that had been building slowly in Ryan broke the surface. "That's not how it is! Whatever you tell her, she responds to *me*."

The spirit's laughter rang through the circle of trees. "You can handle it. Just remember whose girl she is, that's all. I'm losing concentration. Gotta go."

Ryan swore, "Damn it, I told you, I won't play this game . . ." He felt a sudden shift in the air around him, and an odd silence. Sanders got up from his comfortable place on the grass. Ryan paused. "Craig?"

Only a weak echo responded, as if from far away. "See ya."

Aching with exhaustion from lack of sleep and the emotional overload, Ryan sat on a swing in a spray of moonlight and stared out into the shadows with Sanders's head resting on his lap.

If he could keep Emily away from the island, he would, but there was no way to do that. If Craig insisted on keeping up this deceit, Ryan had no choice but to try to tell her the truth. He had to tell her the truth, anyway. Whether Craig liked it or not.

"How the devil am I going to explain it?" he asked his dog. Sanders looked up at him with sad yellow eyes that seemed to reflect Ryan's own thoughts. *It's too late. The damage is already done.*

8

RYAN WOKE at dawn with his head aching and a dog's nose in his face. Exhausted after a short, restless sleep, he lay for a few moments, absently petting Sanders, aware of the scent of Emily's perfume on his pillow and thinking about the hollow ache inside him.

It was the familiar ache. He had lost every person he deeply cared about, and he would lose Emily, too, if he hadn't already. Last night should never have happened. He'd been unable to resist her, but it would never work. City girl, country guy... different life-styles altogether...

Ryan raised up, brushing his thick hair from his eyes. He sat on the edge of the bed holding his head in his hands while Sanders licked his arms. Numbly he remembered Emily's passion, and later Emily's hurt and anger. She had every reason to be upset... somehow "upset" wasn't the right word for what she thought, and felt. It was Craig's fault this happened. Craig had said he loved her, and it was Craig she'd been responding to last night, just as he said.

Damn. How had Craig managed to charm her so completely? He wasn't even... Ryan shook his head. He wasn't even alive. Alive or not, why didn't Craig know better than to do this?

For a fractured moment, time went away for him, with the urge to burst into Craig's room and roust him out of bed as he had done so often, and confront him for his latest crazy scheme. His room, across the hall, with identical twin beds, was still untouched, still exactly as it had been the morning Craig left it and never came home again. Ryan hadn't been able to make himself go in there; he couldn't stand the memories or the sting of his own tears. And he didn't know—then or now—what to do with his anger.

Ryan was wrung out; the past months he'd suffered more emotional pain than he could tolerate. He would have to let go of his feelings for Emily; there was no other way to protect himself from getting hurt. And protecting them both from Craig's jealousy. He had no idea what Craig might do with his jealousy. With a giant sigh, he forced himself up, while he ruffled the fur of the dog's head, saying, "Love isn't worth it, Sanders."

Yet he already missed her smile.

He was working an early shift. It was not yet six o'clock when he got into his car, without even the benefit of coffee. The dispatcher always had coffee at the office. As he drove, anger gnawed at the raw edges of his frustration. What Craig was doing was damn unfair to Emily; it was a selfish trick, and the fallout from it had only begun. He had to think of some way to explain this to her and get Craig to listen to reason. This morning, though, he was at a loss to think of a reasonable way to approach either one of them.

THE SUN rising over the trees of Wildwood shone across the misty meadow and through her bedroom window, into Emily's eyes. From a dream of seeing everything double—people, houses, even herself in the mirror— she woke slowly, relieved it was only a dream. Reality crept in slowly. It wasn't a dream; it really happened. The man she loved was two men and she hadn't been able to tell them apart.

Now that she knew, though, she could identify which was which. Couldn't she?

But what if she hadn't accidentally learned the truth and the charade had gone on? Would she have given herself to both men, not knowing? Such a thing was unthinkable! Yet it could easily have happened. And if Ryan had allowed it, then he didn't deserve to be loved by any woman. No! He wouldn't have! But he knew what was going on. He slept with her knowing his brother had pretended to be him.

Hell. This was where she left off last night. Thoughts of their lovemaking came and went like swirls, sending her into a strange, floating kind of high. Then the next moment, she would crash back to reality, remembering the photos of identical twins. What a fool she'd made of herself!

Damn them. She was going to get the satisfaction of confronting Craig Callister and telling him she knew who he was and that their adolescent game was over. They were going to realize they'd picked the wrong victim this time.

Angrily, Emily threw off the sheet and went to the window to see how high the sun had risen. At just that moment the sheriff's car was pulling out of Callister's driveway. Ryan was going to work early. Good! That would give her a chance to look for his brother, wherever he hung out. Did he work on the farm? Why had no one mentioned him? The bedroom she hadn't looked in might have been his, and he might even have been in there . . . no, not at that hour. The only place she knew where he could be was where he'd been before.

First, though, she needed coffee for a jump start. Barefoot, in her shortie pajamas, she padded down to the kitchen where Aunt Eve, in a crisp yellow summer dress trimmed in white eyelet, and an apron printed with pink and yellow roses, was stirring pancake batter. She was even wearing rouge this morning.

"You don't look very good, dear," Eve observed cheerfully. "Were you up terribly late?"

"My allergies kept me awake," she muttered, thinking it wasn't a lie; she was allergic to men named Callister. Aunt Eve knew Ryan had a twin. If it weren't for the dumb feud and Eve's refusal to talk about that family, she'd have found out a long time ago . . . probably ten years ago.

"You'll feel better after a good breakfast. I've made hot cinnamon apple topping for our pancakes. Ralph's coming over—"

"Not for *breakfast?*"

Eve smiled. "No, I've made breakfast for you and me. But he's coming soon to stake out an area for a clubhouse. He's so sweet, Emily. You'll like him when you get to know him. He brought me flowers last night."

Fear jabbed Emily. "He's moving right along with his plans, isn't he?"

"I like a decisive man."

Emily wanted to blurt out what Ryan had unearthed about Ralph but it was too soon. There wasn't proof yet and Aunt Eve was not about to take the word of a Callister. But Ralph was closing in on his prey so fast! Finding Craig Callister was going to have to wait. Right now Eve needed her protection.

"Ralph's decisive, all right." She helped herself to freshly brewed coffee. The steaming coffee soothed, but only slightly. Emily flashed back on the moment a few short days ago when she had decided on an extended stay at Appleyard Farm...for the peace, she'd thought. Some peace. This morning things couldn't be crazier.

Eve's gift of flowers remained on the breakfast table, lending a bittersweet scent to the fresh air pouring in through an open window. They had barely finished eating when the sound of truck tires crunched in the driveway.

"He's here!" Aunt Eve beamed, smoothing her hair with one swift nervous gesture.

"Already?" Emily downed another quick swallow of coffee and clicked it down hard on the saucer as she rose. "I've got to get dressed."

Able to move only in slow motion this morning, she showered and dressed in shorts and walking shoes and braided her hair into a single braid. By the time she got to the back porch, the field to the east was dotted with bright splashes of red, which she realized were small flags on stakes. Eve was standing hugging her arms at the edge of a flower bed watching Ralph pace off the ground and plant his flags.

The nerve! Emily thought, feeling her ears redden with rage. She rushed off the porch and came up, breathlessly, alongside her aunt.

Eve turned. "Oh, Emily, isn't it exciting? It's the beginning of our resort."

Emily's teeth clenched. "I doubt if it's even legal, Aunt Eve."

She smiled. "Ralph is going to take care of any legal requirements. He knows all about that sort of thing."

Ralph, having seen Emily approach, waved and tromped over to greet her. "Good morning, Emily girl!" he sang. "How does it look?"

"Like trouble," she said. "This resort idea is going to ruin not only Appleyard Farm but this whole part of the valley."

He puckered his lips, feigning shock. "Whoa. Do I detect a sour note?"

Detect? Emily squinted. "It looks like the thing is going to be forced on us whether we like the idea or not."

Ralph waved his fistful of little flags at her. "I seem to be confused about who this farm belongs to. I thought Eve was the owner and you were a visitor."

Eve gasped. "Emily is my family!" she cried. "And if we're going to make these big changes, we should talk them over with her."

"We did talk them over," Ralph lied. "Is it my fault Emily is never around? This is your land and your decision, Eve."

"Not entirely. It will be Emily's farm someday. She's my only heir."

Emily felt the boring glare of Ralph Peckham's black eyes, and she remembered the evil she had seen in them.

Nothing would incense him more than what Eve had just said.

Emily asked, "What's your enormous hurry, anyhow?" She knew the answer, of course. The faster he got his claws in, the less likely he was to be stopped...by anybody who wanted to stop him, including Eve. And Emily herself. And Ryan and Craig Callister. As far as Ralph and Eve knew, their next-door neighbors had no idea this was going on and wouldn't know until the gun club "resort" was a reality and the guns were going nonstop. The sheriff not only knew, but he was also fighting mad. Ralph was in for a shock.

"Eve and I have lots of plans," Ralph said, ignoring her question and slipping an arm around Eve's shoulders. "A lot of which might be personal."

"I have no secrets from my niece," Eve said. She smiled at Emily. "I do want to talk to you, dear."

This sounded bad. Very bad. Fighting back an urge to strangle the man, Emily said viciously, "Well, when Ralph is through messing up your property with his stupid flags, let me know. We'll talk then, just the two of us."

She turned and walked over to the barn and sat down on the sloping wooden ramp at the doorway, to watch Ralph's movements from a distance. She'd had so many thoughts in the past few days of staying, of living at Appleyard Farm, but the idea seemed destined not to be. She couldn't live here if Eve married Peckham, God forbid. No way could she live in the same house with him. And her dream romance with her childhood love had turned into a nightmare of mistaken identity. Yet she was falling in love with this farm, and it would be hard to leave.

Sanders appeared from a nearby grove and trotted up to say hello, an obvious social call that surprised her. "Hey, I thought you'd been taught never to come back of the enemy lines, Sanders." He must have sensed that the danger was gone, although he sat close to her, eyeing the man in the field with what Emily was certain was suspicion.

She gave him a hug. Anyway, the Callisters' dog liked her. Too bad he couldn't talk. The two sat on the ramp for some time, warmed by the morning sun, until Ralph got into his old red pickup and drove away. Eve waved as the truck sped down the gravel road, then turned and waved at Emily. When she stood up, Sanders trotted back into the thick grove and disappeared from sight.

Eve walked toward her. "That dog," she said when she was close enough to be easily heard. "What's it doing here? I'm sure it belongs at Wildwood. It might be vicious."

"He's friendly," Emily assured her. They fell into step together, walking toward the back porch, where they sat down.

"Oh, Emily, I'm so happy, so very, very happy. Ralph has asked me to be his wife."

Emily closed her eyes and saw the color orange behind her lids. "Why didn't you tell me this at breakfast?"

Eve hadn't stopped smiling since the truck pulled away. "Oh, he hadn't asked me then, although he was hinting at it. Only now. Just now."

"He asked you just now? After you said that about my being your only relative so I'd inherit the farm?"

She nodded. "He said he hadn't realized I had only one relative and he didn't want me to be lonely when you leave. Isn't that thoughtful and sweet?" She rested her hand on her chest and sighed happily. "Actually, dear, it was what I had wanted to talk to you about. I thought it might be nice if you had some interest in this new business we're starting. Since you'll eventually inherit the farm—"

"Aunt Eve, if you marry Ralph, it'll be his farm. And he'd inherit it, should anything ever happen to you."

"Oh my, perhaps that's true. I was assuming that just the business, the resort, would be his."

"Everything would be his."

"We could work it out, I'm sure, if you are interested in helping with my end of the business. I know it's a very wild idea of mine, and you have a career of your own, but I decided just to ask. Ralph thought we could even start a small inn, and I could run it. But I'd need help, of course." She seemed flustered now. "Oh, I'm being a silly goose, aren't I? To even think such a thing?"

Emily reached for her hand. "No, Aunt Eve, it's not silly at all. I've had thoughts of my own about staying here because I love it. But this gun club is going to ruin your farm. Can't you see that?"

She shook her head. "No, it wouldn't. Ralph says it'll be a lovely place. Just lovely. You'll see. Oh, he is a wonderful man. He truly is."

Emily felt ill. "What did you tell him when he asked you to marry him?"

"I said I'd be honored." She sighed happily again. "Isn't it just so thrilling?"

"Aunt Eve, he...he's..." But she couldn't say it. There was no proof he was a con man and the accusation would only distance her from Eve, which would be the worst thing right now, just what Ralph wanted. Obviously, he was threatened by Emily, so he had jumped the gun. "He's...rushing you," she said. "Leo has died so recently. What will people think?"

"I mentioned that, and he says he doesn't care what people think. He only knows how much he loves me." She raised both arms. "A wonderful man loves me. Loves *me* and wants to marry me. I never thought it could ever happen to me. It's so romantic. Oh, please be happy for me, Emily. To be able to share my happiness with you means so much."

"I want...I want you to be happy more than anything," Emily said huskily, feeling a terrible ache in her heart. "But surely you needn't *rush* into this. I mean, there are plans to make and—"

"Oh, yes, and you're here to help me. It's like a dream, isn't it?"

Dreams sure did have a way of turning sour around here, Emily thought.

"I'm going to plan a little announcement party. Just my very best friends. All those who knew Leo will understand. They'll be thrilled for me, too. Would you like another cup of coffee, dear? A cookie, maybe?"

She shook her head. "I feel like a walk, Aunt Eve. It's such a pretty morning."

"It's a sensational morning!" Eve began to hum.

From halfway across the lawn, heading toward the path by the lake, Emily could hear her singing full voice.

THE ISLAND was unnaturally still. Night frogs were silent now. Some of the morning mist still hung in the shadows. Leaves soaked from last night's rain glistened in the sun. Along the path were lacy webs beaded with sparkling drops of water. Morning flowers had opened their petals to the light. There were no footprints in the sand, which meant he probably wasn't here. Well, he wouldn't hang out here all the time.

When the eerie feeling of being watched came upon her, she blamed it on squirrels in the high branches. But the shadows moved erratically as they always did here and branches bent against wind that wasn't blowing. In her wet swimsuit, Emily made her way along a grown-over path toward the center.

"Craig?" she called, startled by the echo of her own voice. "Craig? Are you here?"

"Hi, Emily!" The voice came from directly behind her and made her jump.

"You startled me!" she scolded before she'd had time to register that he'd answered to his own name.

"Sorry. I didn't mean to."

He was smiling, so handsome in the shadowy sunlight, his looks distracted her. It was like looking at a painting the way his eyes reflected the light and the way sun gleamed on his hair.

She stared into his eyes, noting how different they were from Ryan's. "You are Craig, aren't you?"

His silence told her he must have responded to his own name automatically, without thinking.

"Well, aren't you?"

"Yeah. I guess Ryan told you, huh?"

"No. I found out quite on my own. If you must know how, I saw the photos of the two of you. It was a shock. I thought I was seeing double." She looked squarely at him. "You wanted me to think you were Ryan. Why would you do that?"

His strange eyes widened with innocence. "It started before...when we were kids, letting you think there was only one of us. It was just meant as a joke. We were going to tell you sometime."

"But you didn't. Even now."

"We were fighting over you, Emily. We both fell in love with you. That hasn't changed."

This confession, because it sounded sincere, caused Emily to tremble. She was stunned into silence. They both loved her, all those years ago? And now...?

Gradually, as she stood in the dappled sunshine of the island, what had made absolutely no sense began to show a hideous picture to her. Was he saying they both wanted her so they were going to share her?

Words tumbled almost involuntarily from her mouth. "You decided you'd both pretend to be one guy so I wouldn't have to . . . choose?"

He made an attempt at defending himself. "It wasn't planned that way."

"You made a fool of me, Craig. Ryan . . . was . . . I thought . . . I mean . . ." Tears of anger and hurt threatened to rise again; she fought them back out of pride, but the trembling in her voice betrayed any resolve not to show her pain and embarrassment. She didn't want to admit to him that she and Ryan had made love last night because of what *Craig* had said to her. He'd know soon enough, through Ryan, but she couldn't say it, facing him.

He was frowning now, looking at her in a way he never had. The expression on his face reminded her of Ryan's last night. Why the hell should they look so upset? She was the victim here. Angry, she said, "I wanted to find you this morning to let you know your stupid game is over. I'm not playing the part of fool anymore. Ryan is still playing, making excuses. He didn't want me to confront you. He even went so far as to try to make me believe you were dead. How low can you sink?"

She tried to ignore his gaze, so intense it seemed as if her pain had become his own.

"You got hurt over this . . ." he mumbled in a monotone as if the possibility had never occurred to him.

"What did you expect, when you—" His stare was so unnerving she had to turn away. "When he—" She stopped herself, then blurted out the worst of it. "Ryan telling me such a hideous lie—"

Craig took a small step closer. His voice became soft, full of concern. "He wasn't lying, Emily. I am dead."

She glared at him, her anger rising higher. "Just keep it up!" she raged. "Maybe both of you ought to be committed! I should have known better than to try to talk to either of you!"

She turned away from him, but suddenly he was standing in front of her. For a wild second she thought they were both there, one in front and one behind. But no, it was Craig. How had he done that?

He said, "I know it's hard to believe, but it's true. It seems like no time to me, but I've been dead for a year and a half—earth years—and I thought I was adjusting to the change until I saw that you were here again and I came back . . . materialized, if you want to call it that . . . to see you. I didn't want to give up the chance to be with you again. When I said I'd waited for you to return, it was the truth."

Emily felt a tremor of fear, not knowing where it came from. From living a nightmare, maybe. Was he insane?

"Don't look at me like that," he pleaded.

"Like *what?*"

"Like you were seeing a ghost." He began to chuckle. "Damn it, I guess technically I am, whether I like the label or not. I was going to tell you sometime, I just—"

"Craig . . ." Her voice cracked with anger. "Stop this . . ." She turned to run, but forced herself to merely walk away.

"You don't believe me." He was beside her now.

"Of course not. I can see that you're a man the same as Ryan. Two identical crackpots."

"But he can touch you and I can't."

She stopped, thinking back. It was true, he hadn't touched her, and she hadn't felt the heat near him, either, the heat her body always generated when Ryan was close.

"And yes, you can see me," he was continuing, "but you can't touch me." He extended his right arm. "Here. Go ahead. Try to touch me."

She started walking again, beginning to feel queasy. "I told you I'm not playing anymore."

He pushed the arm against her hand, but she could feel nothing. Her fingers went right through his arm. She gasped and drew back in alarm.

"I'm only spirit," he said. "Only an illusion of the physical. Even Ryan can't see me . . . he can only hear me. That's because I'm dead. By earth definition, anyway. There isn't really such a thing as death, except by earth definition . . ."

His prattling was audible to her and she could discern the words, yet their meaning was impossible to assimilate. *I'm only spirit . . . dead . . .*

No! her logical mind screamed. *It's another trick! Illusion . . . he said the word himself.*

"Leave me alone!" she demanded in a quaking voice. "Just get away from me and leave me alone!" She broke into a run, heading toward the swings and the path that led out. He called her back but she wouldn't listen. His voice seemed to be floating just above her.

"Don't run off," he was pleading. "You know there's nothing to fear from me. Damn it, I can't help it if I'm not still alive like you . . ."

"You're not sane like me, either," she muttered aloud, ducking under the bramble wall to reach the safety of the cove, knowing he probably couldn't hear the insult. "At least I was sane when I came to Phantom Ridge . . ."

She swam hard until she reached the shore, climbed up breathlessly and sat down in a circle of slender trees, a circle so narrow she could touch each tree around her. The trees closed their high branches over her, protectively, as if it were safe to think here, to try to understand . . .

It was true, she couldn't touch him. Nor could she feel his touch. It was true, he just materialized mysteriously each time she showed up on the island. Materialized . . . his word. Trying to catch her breath, Emily was shaking all over. He had been in front of her, behind her, above her, all at once. His voice had a strange echo, and his eyes were too silver to reflect any colors. He had said the words so softly, yet so matter-of-factly, "*I am dead.*"

"God help me," she whispered to the silent trees as her intuition took over where reason would not. Ryan wouldn't lie about his twin's death. And no living man would claim to be dead. With her head buried in her arms, Emily sat trembling, remembering the touch she couldn't feel, too stunned to cry, too stunned to think.

Ghost. He had called himself a ghost. Her head began to throb. She had encountered the ghost of Ryan's brother? How could it be?

How could it not?

She sat for a long time, staring out toward the strange little island. All the confusion came crystal clear to her: the spirit of Craig Callister had reached through to her. She had nothing to fear from him. Nothing. How could he harm her? He couldn't even touch her.

Steadying herself with the tree trunks, Emily got to her feet on trembling knees. She walked the short distance back to the shore and stood looking over at the island hidden behind a wall of thorns and roses, so still and peaceful in the summer sun. She gazed at the shaded island with tears clouding her eyes, tears formed from pity. How awful to be dead and want to be alive again . . .

The pond grass under her feet gave way to sandy bottom as she waded in, scarcely feeling the cool rush of water around her legs. Then around her shoulders.

She swam back.

9

EMILY CRAWLED soaking wet out of the opening in the thicket and into the stillness that was part of the mystery of Pillywiggin Island. She stood shivering with the wall of wild roses at her back and timidly whispered his name.

Craig appeared out of nowhere, standing a short distance away. They gazed at each other in silence. Emily studied him, overcome by the beauty and the mystery of him. At last she asked in a whispery voice, "Why didn't you tell me before?"

He smiled. "You mean like, 'Hi, Emily, my name's Craig. I know I look just like Ryan but I'm actually a ghost.'"

She took several deep breaths, blinking repeatedly, trying to make this conversation real. Was he the reason Ryan didn't want to bring her over? She asked shakily, "Does Ryan know you're here? On the island?"

"He does now. He came last night, finally. I had wanted to talk to him, clear up some stuff."

"He didn't know before?"

"Not till last night. We talked about you, Emily. I told him you were mine."

She gasped. *"Yours?"*

"My girl. I threatened to make trouble."

"You made trouble, all right."

He reached out as if to touch her. "My sweet girl. Am I forgiven? Please forgive me. I didn't mean to hurt you. It's kind of hard to love you from where I am now, I mean in any way that you can respond to." He drew nearer, his eyes showing a shine of silver. "Pretend I'm as alive as you. I do love you and I want your love. Yesterday you loved me."

Tears spilled from her eyes. "Yes, I did."

"I'm still me."

"Yes . . ." she conceded, thinking that in the way he meant, it was true.

"And I need your love. You won't turn away from me, will you? Just because I'm not Ryan?"

She swallowed. *Turn away from him?* How could she do that, when she had met him as a friend and wanted to be his friend, and when her heart had answered with a quickened beat both times he said he loved her? There were many kinds of love. To turn away from the ghost was to turn away from someone who . . . who cared for her, and whom she cared for in return. She swallowed. "No, of course I won't."

"Thank the angels," he said. "I'm your friend, believe that. I'll watch over you. I'll get better at it as time goes on. I'm still adjusting."

She listened in amazement, her heart going out to him.

"It's hard letting go," he confessed. "Especially if those I love and the home I love are threatened."

"Threatened?" she asked, groping for anything familiar.

"I mean the gun club that threatens the peace of Wildwood. What's happening with that?"

Her heart beat faster. *Was there any way a ghost could help?* "It's horrid. Ralph Peckham intends to marry my aunt to get her farm and then he'll do whatever he wants with it."

"Ryan will be mad as hell and out to stop it."

"If he can, he will." She fell into step beside him and they walked toward the island's center. "Really, Craig, should you be saying the word hell?"

He grinned. "Probably not. When I get mad I get careless."

She noted how easily he laughed, much more easily than Ryan, and she wondered if he'd always been that way, even before . . .

"Ryan is trying to find a way to stop Peckham," she said. "But he can't find a legal way. I can't influence Aunt Eve when she's in this state of bliss. I swear, love is a form of insanity."

"The best plan would be to expose him for what he is—a thief."

"He's an *experienced* thief. Clever and careful."

"Then you'll have to set him up."

Emily bit her lip. "How?"

"Why not plant some stolen goods in his car and turn him in to the law."

"Ryan's the law. He'd never go for it."

Craig laughed. "Nope, he wouldn't. So don't tell him you did it."

The thought was horrifying. "Surely you can come up with something better than this!"

"I'll work on it," he promised. "But it sounds like we don't have much time."

"Not much time at all, and I'm desperate."

"Stolen goods . . . it'd work."

They had reached the old bench. Emily, still feeling weak in the knees, was eager to sit down. The ghost sat beside her. She stared at the ground, noting that his bare feet kicked up no dirt and left no footprints. Odd she hadn't noticed before . . .

She said thoughtfully, "Craig, you're in the spirit world now. Doesn't that mean you can know things . . . see things we can't? Like even the future?"

He shook his head. "That's a misconception. I'm still me. It's easier to learn things here, see beyond earth things, so I'm told, once we really make that break away from human emotions, but it doesn't happen all at once. I've got . . . all these feelings for you, so I'm earth-connected. Someday, supposedly, I'll get better at seeing further, and knowing beyond. I wish I could for your sake, so I could help you more with this Peckham problem."

"So you can't predict outcomes any more than I can."

"No. But I do know this much—you shouldn't be afraid to take a chance because Ryan will protect you if anything goes wrong. He's not easygoing like I am . . . was. If he goes after this Peckham, he'll get him. Believe me, he'll get him."

"But meantime, there could be a marriage."

"No," he answered. "Meantime we're going to think of a way to stall for time." He turned. "We'd better keep our friendship a secret from Ryan."

"Why?"

"Think about it. He'll be mad as hell at both of us, but especially me. Just for now, anyway, promise me you won't tell him we have this . . . pact."

"Pact?"

"Pact to stop the gun club. Pact to love each other..."

"Craig . . ."

"As friends," he stated. "As special friends."

This didn't feel right to Emily. She objected, "But I don't like secrets. Secrets are what started—"

"We'll work it out with him," Craig promised. "But first give us some time."

Unease settled over her. "Time . . . ?"

"Well . . . I need some time to mull over this Peckham problem, for one thing. I'm not restrained by legalities, unlike Ryan."

Ryan. Memories of last night began darting around her like beams of dusty sunlight. *Ryan . . .* The thought of him, and of them together, warmed Emily to her toes. He hadn't known what she was so hysterical about...he hadn't understood. Neither had she, when she had run away, ignoring his pleas.

Emily rose, still shaky. "I have to get back!"

Craig stood, but didn't follow as she headed for the path, suddenly in a hurry. "See ya," he said.

Momentarily Emily closed her eyes in pain when she heard those words from long ago...and so far away... "See ya," she called back.

Drying off at the water's edge, Emily was tense with anxiety. It felt as though her body, as well as her dreams, were shadow-bruised. She struggled to try to balance the uneven truths—Ryan had not told her about his twin, but he hadn't lied to her, nor tried to trick her.

The sweet, transparent days had gone, and been replaced by something she could scarcely understand. But the mysteries of Craig were already out of focus. For the taste of last night's passion—like the taste of honey—remained, overpowering her other senses. She had to see Ryan! Evening was too far away. There was probably little chance of catching him in the office, and even if she did, they couldn't talk there. Emily combed her wet hair, slid the comb into her pocket and started across the meadow toward Wildwood. The house might be unlocked, and she could leave a note saying she would come back after he got home tonight.

She reached the top of the meadow, from where the green sloped gently down to the farmhouses. To her surprise, the sheriff's car was turning off the main road into Ryan's driveway. Emily waved and began to run.

Ryan didn't see her. He stepped out, greeting Sanders, who was always there to meet him. Sanders didn't stop to be petted; he had a message to convey. Tail wagging, he jumped and lunged toward the slope. Ryan squinted through the sunlight.

"Emily?"

He started toward her, and held out his arms. In seconds, she was there, breathless, panting, singing his name.

"Ryan! What are you doing home in the middle of the afternoon?"

"I took time off to make a private phone call." He hugged her uncertainly. When she returned the embrace, his arms tightened around her, and for several seconds, they held each other in silence. She felt so warm in his arms.

"To you . . ." he said, after a time.

"What?"

"I came back to phone you . . . if I didn't see you outside anywhere, to ask if you'd see me tonight. Will you?"

"Yes."

They walked to the side porch and sat in the cushioned swing. Ryan took her hand. "Emily, I should have told you sooner about Craig . . . I'd been trying to . . . to think how. I just . . . I . . . I'm glad to see you're calmer than when you left last night."

She glanced at him, then away. "I apologize for not believing you when you told me your twin brother was dead. I found out you were telling the truth."

"It's no secret. Everybody in Phantom Ridge knows."

She nodded. "But I didn't realize you had a brother and I couldn't understand why you never told me. It smacked of secrets and conspiracy."

Ryan winced. "Yeah, I can see why you'd think that. I had no reason not to tell you, except that I didn't like talking about it. I'm not good at dealing with . . . with his being gone. Time is supposed to heal everything, but it doesn't. Believe me, it doesn't."

Her heart went out to him. The very mention of Craig brought pain to Ryan's eyes. Losing his brother had been a kind of hell he hadn't been able to handle. The suffering was still there.

"I'm sorry for your loss," she said softly.

"And I'm sorry for the misunderstanding."

Emily was hesitant to mention the ghost, but it was more awkward not to. She said, "I knew it wasn't you on the island. Craig is still there, isn't he?"

Ryan looked at her, frowning. "I don't know how to explain it."

She tried to smile. "And if you had tried to explain last night, I wouldn't have believed you."

"Last night I didn't know," he said. "After you left, I went to the island and talked to him myself." Ryan swallowed. The pain hadn't left his eyes. "I can't explain any of it."

"Then don't try." She looked away, at the sunlight tangled in the branches of the shade trees near the porch. "Ryan, are you sorry last night happened? Between us?"

"Yeah. It was a mistake."

She felt a black cloud descend over her . . . the black cloud that was somehow a part of him. She asked, "Why?"

The question surprised him. "I took advantage of you, Emily. I'm not proud of that. In spite of what some women think, not all guys make a game of . . . sex. We both know now it was just an impulse—"

"Was it?" She interrupted softly. "Then it was a pretty strong impulse."

This brought only the hint of a smile. "I won't deny that, but the point is, I don't believe in a fling just for its own sake, and I doubt if you do, either."

The hurt was eating her flesh, a slow wound he didn't seem to realize he was inflicting. "I didn't know a fling was all it was."

His brow wrinkled. "What else, Emily? You're here for a short visit—"

"I had thought of staying a lot longer."

His head jerked up. "Are you?"

She sighed deeply. "If my aunt married Ralph Peckham, I can't. I'll have to go. But I'm doing everything in my power to stop that marriage. I like...it here." She looked over at him, at his handsome face in the dusty sunlight, and the ache was deep in her. Last night meant little to him? Was that what he was saying? It was a mistake? While she, sitting here watching his eyes and his hands and his lips as he talked, had begun to ache for him as she'd never ached before. Knowing what it was like to lie with him . . . to touch him, to be touched by him, just the knowing, the memory, caused her blood to heat and her limbs to tremble. How could he call it a *mistake?*

He was studying the changes in her eyes. "Emily, what's the matter?"

She squinted back. "What's the matter with you?"

"What do you mean?"

Her lips trembled. "Last night was something very special to me, and I thought to you. How could you call it a mistake?"

He swallowed. "You thought I was somebody else. You thought Craig was...I mean, you thought I was..." He shook his head. "You know what I mean."

She raised her hand in the air. "I knew damn well who you were...and who you are!" She closed her eyes. "All right, I'll admit I encouraged you, believing you said you loved me when you hadn't said it and you're saying now that you don't. And I feel pretty stupid because of it. But I also know how you looked at me. Damn it, I see how you look at me now! I know what I felt when I saw my reflection in your eyes. So what is this really about, Ryan? Why don't you level with me and tell me why you're trying to break off our relationship?"

"I'm not trying to do that!"

"Well, you're doing an excellent job of it."

Ryan slid his arm around her shoulders and drew her closer to him. "Emily, you matter to me . . . you matter too much, that's the problem. I don't want to invest in caring too much for you and then have you walk out of my life. I don't have the emotional stamina for it right now."

"Maybe I don't, either."

"Then why make it harder for ourselves?"

She gazed at him for a long time, listening to the sounds of a hot summer afternoon . . . the golden glow of sunlight splashing over the trees and the flowers and the fields . . . the quiet . . . the peace . . . the smell of fresh air mixed with honeysuckle . . . his world . . . better than any other she knew.

Emily asked softly, "Would you let me walk away?"

The question threw him. What did her walking away have to do with him? He exhaled a great breath. "I couldn't stop you. I have nothing to offer you that would make you happy."

"What a strange thing to say, Ryan, when I've been sitting here thinking how much you have . . . such a beautiful property, such a beautiful world."

Ryan smiled. "Yeah, I've got Wildwood. But you're used to so much more."

She took a deep breath. "Oh, Ryan, get real. I live on a teacher's salary. In a small apartment in Chicago, shared with a TWA flight attendant who hasn't the faintest idea how to wash a dish and can't sleep without the television blasting. When she's in town I sometimes go to the library just for a little peace."

He took this in with shock. Ryan didn't know just how he had pictured her life, but certainly nothing like she was describing. He said, "Does that make you a gypsy, then?"

Emily laughed. "Well, yeah, I'm something of a wanderer. I like to go other places, see what some of the world is like. The crowded city closes up on me and makes me nervous."

"Are you going to England this fall to teach?"

"I suppose so. Unless I can somehow stop this wedding."

"I don't have much desire to travel," he said.

It translated, *We don't have anything in common and we both know it.* The comment also translated, *I'm not ready or willing to invest in any emotional involvement right now. That's what I'm trying to tell you.*

She heard him loud and clear.

She could say, *I wouldn't have a desire to travel, either, if I lived in a place like this . . .* But no, it would sound as if she were pleading, and she wasn't about to wish herself on a guy who wasn't willing to love her the way she loved him . . . the way she deserved to be loved. Ryan had been through such emotional turmoil, he didn't seem to know what he wanted. Except maybe to be primarily and adequately alone. She felt desperate to change his mood tonight.

So in keeping with what came most natural to her, Emily leaned on the table, chin on palm, and launched into the sport of mockery. "No desire to travel? What do you have desire for? Never mind, don't strain your brain thinking of a cute answer. I found out last night what you desire. I have memorized what you desire."

Amusement shone in his eyes. "You're a talented tease."

She had nothing to lose by teasing him. She understood Ryan so much better now—understood his moods and the sadness that sometimes shone in his eyes. She understood why he was afraid of losing if he allowed himself to love. She understood why he had almost forgotten how to play. And she understood how much he wanted her.

"Yep, I admit to being a tease. And do you know what I'd tease you about if I were to stay around here, in your world?"

"I'm afraid to ask."

"Twin beds." She smiled. "I'd tease you about having twin beds in your room . . . if I were to stay."

It was impossible to tell from his expression whether he was on the verge of laughter or not. She couldn't guess what he was thinking. She asked, "Why *do* you have twin beds?"

"They were always there, in that room."

"But haven't you thought of getting a more comfortable—" Emily stopped. She was beginning to embarrass herself. It was something she actually wondered about, but it was coming out as if she was obsessed with beds.

Ryan propped his feet on the wooden table in front of the swing. "Okay, I thought about it. The truth is, I've often thought I should move into the room my mother had. It's bigger and has the fireplace and a larger bed. I just never got around to it. Those changes sound easier than they actually are." He looked at her, his arm still around her shoulders. "Or maybe I just never had enough incentive. You're saying my bed was too small last night . . . ?"

She wanted to keep up the teasing game, but it was too frustrating, because she couldn't tell what Ryan was really thinking. Was he just being nice to her now because he knew she'd been tricked? A glaze of tears formed in her eyes. She whispered, "Last night . . . wasn't a mistake."

He hugged her closer against his body and answered softly. "You can get under my skin, Emily. Nobody else could ever do that. You know how to live for the moment, and I've always had a hard time doing that."

"What's wrong with living for the moment, Ryan? If that's what we choose to do?"

"Do you? Choose to?"

She felt the warmth of his hand on hers and snuggled against him. "Yes. I choose to."

This beautiful woman was offering him the moment, as she had done last night, because she wanted to . . . because she cared for him. He was not the kind of fool who could turn away from a gift of love, nor was he strong enough, because Emily was warmth and softness . . . treasures he had all but forgotten. Treasures she offered so generously. Her warmth . . . her softness . . .

He was overwhelmed by the pleadings of his heart . . . and of his body. He needed her so much . . .

He turned his body into hers, kissed her—lightly at first, then deeper—until she was trembling.

"You're right, beautiful lady. I was being an idiot, thinking it wasn't me you wanted . . ."

"Stop thinking so much, Ryan . . ."

I'm doing it again! Emily thought with panic. *Tempting, beguiling, luring. Damn.* It was his fault for being so handsome that it was a shock each time she saw him, his fault for having eyes bluer than the sky, for talking to her in a voice as smooth as black velvet, for heating her entire body with a mere touch of his hand. For dazzling her sense and her senses with his sensual kiss. Now that she knew him, knew his body, his moans of pleasure, his mesmerizing eyes, she couldn't help herself, not any more now than she could last night. When every fiber of instinct told her he wanted her just as much, there was no fighting the sensations of desire that overcame her at the thought of making love with him again.

And his kiss said he wanted her. Whether he wanted to want her or not, he did.

"Emily . . ." he whispered. "Tonight . . ."

She wasn't sure what he'd just said. Her head was spinning. "What?"

His breath was hot against her cheek as he spoke, holding her. "Tonight. If I stay off my car radio any longer, Beebe is going to be out here looking for me. I have to go back to work. Come tonight . . ." His voice trailed off. He kissed her again. "Tonight there is something I want to show you."

She gazed into his eyes and saw they had changed; they'd softened, as if they were filled with fairy dust. "Ryan . . . what are you thinking?"

"About us," he said. "About living for . . . tonight."

SANDERS STOOD beside her watching Ryan's car pull away. He walked with her to the Appleyard buildings, where he ran ahead, and circled back with one of Ralph Peckham's red land markers in his mouth.

"Good boy!" she exclaimed as she grabbed the little flag and threw it for him to retrieve. When he brought it back, she put it into her pocket. Not to have the fun cut off so suddenly, Sanders did what she expected and went to get another.

And another. And another.

Before long, the field Ralph had staked out for his club was a smooth meadow again, and a pile of tiny flags was hidden under a log deep in the woods. There were no human footprints at the scene of the crime. Emily was back to worrying about what was going to happen to her beloved aunt.

Aunt Eve's car wasn't in the garage. She found a note on the kitchen counter saying Eve had gone into the village "to do some shopping." Frustrated, she went back out into the sunshine and busied herself pulling weeds between the neat rows of Eve's summer garden. Her mind wasn't on weeds, though. She had completely forgotten to tell Ryan the gun club had reached the panic stage. It was something he needed to know.

Sanders showed up again, still wanting her company and wanting to play. He ran along the garden fence, sniffing, following one scent trail, then another. He disappeared, then returned with something bright in his mouth to resume their earlier game. "What've you got this time?" she asked. He dropped a little yellow bonnet in her hand.

"Aunt Eve's goose hat! Sanders, you little thief! Aunt Eve would kill you." She leaned close. "You'd better not get caught stealing *these*."

The words echoed back. *Stolen goods.* Just what the ghost had ordered! It was a sign, her answer. The idea was nuts, but here beside her, licking her hand, was a professional, willing thief, an accomplice. Emily thought about the red truck with the sprung door that Ralph never closed when he parked. What could be easier!

Of course, one little goose hat wasn't enough. They needed more. Sliding the hat into her pocket, Emily hurried across to her car. "Come on, Sanders, let's case the neighborhood!"

He jumped eagerly into her car. "Whatever you do," she said, starting the engine, "don't tell Ryan what we're up to. He'd have to arrest you instead of Ralph." She broke out in nervous giggles.

Half a mile down the road, she slowed. "On the left, Sanders! Goose in Fourth of July outfit!" The dog leaned his head out of the window, then looked back at her with eyes full of joyous mischief. She grinned at him, certain he understood the game.

Driving back with her hit list, Emily had a few misgivings. What was she doing, following the advice of a renegade ghost and scheming to make a criminal out of the sheriff's dog!

AUNT EVE pulled into the driveway and started to unload packages. Emily rushed from the garden to help her. "What is all this?"

"Oh, Emily, dear, I found a beautiful wedding dress! I saw it at Maggie Maple's shop months ago and thought it was so beautiful. Maggie even had a little hat to match. I can't wait to show you!"

Emily was glad Eve had parked in the back where she couldn't see the bareheaded goose. She followed her through the kitchen and into the dining room. "Isn't this rushing things too much?"

Eve opened a box, rustling the tissue paper inside. "I suppose some people might think so. But it's not as if I were a young woman, dear. Why must one postpone happiness just for what others might say?" She pulled out a cloud blue chiffon dress, fitted at the waist and trimmed in cream-colored lace with long lace sleeves. "Just look! It's the prettiest dress I ever saw!" Eve Stark held the dress in front of her and began to waltz in circles, singing, "Oh . . . la la la . . . how we danced . . . la la la . . . on the night . . ."

Emily could feel nausea rising. Her heart went out to her aunt. To, think, she was scheming to spoil Eve's happiness!

"Imagine how lovely it will be!" Eve was saying, opening another box. "My dear friends there as I walk down the aisle of our little church on the hill. The church will have flowers and white ribbons..." She produced a blue summer hat with a tiny rim and perched it blithely on her head. "And such a handsome groom. He is very handsome, isn't he? I'm so lucky! And isn't it wonderful that you're here to share all this and help me plan?"

I can't stand it! Emily wanted to scream. Instead she cleared her throat to steady her voice and said, "I really think you should wait a proper time, Aunt Eve, I really do. People will think more highly of you."

Eve frowned. "I felt that way, too, dear. I told that very thing to Ralph. He doesn't fashion his life by the opinions of others, he said, and I don't want to, either, but I do have a very respected place in the community. Maybe I'll talk to him about it again. We could wait at least a few weeks, to make it look better."

"Please do. I'd feel so much better, and we'd have time to...to make plans. We must have plans, that's half the fun."

"Maybe you're right, dear," Eve said, setting the hat back in its box. "It would be wonderful fun."

How many people has she told? Emily wondered. She felt very uneasy, guilty. For someone who hated secrets, Emily was embroiled in them. Damn. She wanted to tell Aunt Eve right here and now that she and Ryan Callister were lovers—all right, friends—just blurt it out! But she couldn't. No more than she could confess her friendship with the ghost of his brother, who was jealous that Ryan wanted her. Nor could she tell Ryan of her plot to frame Ralph—knowing she and Sanders were going to instigate a crime spree that would be the talk of Phantom Ridge. And tonight . . . an intimate tryst with Ryan. Her heart raced at the thought. What was the allusive something Ryan had promised to show her?

It was hard to imagine that only a few short days ago she had thought it would be just a lovely, peaceful summer in the country.

10

HE LED HER through the deepening shadows and along the edge of the trees. Fireflies twinkled in the night around them.

"They're trying to attract mates," Ryan said.

"Really? That's what they're lighting up about?"

"It always seemed the logical explanation to me."

"A man's version," she chided. "Maybe they're pretending to be stars."

The path opened out at the back of the cove. "The moon is about to rise over the lake," he said. "That's what I wanted to show you. This is the best place to see it."

Once the sun had sunk below the horizon, dark closed in quickly, but Ryan had no trouble seeing in the dark. Stars began winking above them, and below them, in the lake. They sat on a fallen log not far from the water's edge.

"Do you always watch the moon rise?" she asked.

"Usually. When its warm, I like to swim here at night." He pointed to the east where a golden glow was showing near the tops of the trees. "There it is. The first full moon of summer."

The moon rose before their eyes in silence that didn't seem to be silence. Before long the bright globe was a watery lantern in the lake. Stars reflected in the still water and fireflies made the trees sparkle around them. Frogs were chanting loudly from the reeds.

She said, "I hear music, Ryan."

He smiled. "I've never quite figured out what it is. Water lapping against the rushes, maybe. The frogs are so loud, it's hard to tell."

"Fairies singing," she said. The thought had jumped out of nowhere. Fairies lived in the flowers. She pointed to some floating yellow blossoms. "Imagine a moon so bright we can clearly see flowers. The water lilies are blooming."

"They're called spatterdocks, don't ask me why. Have you seen the wild orchids? If you look, you'll find them. They'd look pretty in your hair." He reached up to touch her hair and his hand lingered. He said softly, "Your thoughts are always in your eyes, Emily."

"Thoughts I've never had before."

"Then I'm flattered."

"You should be."

His lips found hers in the moonlight, and lingered, and he held her against his body tightly, so their heartbeats found each other. She felt the hunger of his lips, and of his hands, and of his body. Hunger long denied. Gentle, erotic kisses with a force beyond her wildest imaginings.

"I feel a little dizzy again . . ." she confessed.

"So do I, to be honest." His lips brushed hers. "You do this to me deliberately, Emily, and I can't resist you. Hell, I don't want to resist you." It was true, he knew. Her draw was too powerful. Her beauty cast a spell on him . . . the beauty of her face, her eyes, her body, her heart . . . She was so open, so sincere, so unashamed of her feelings for him. In these magical moments, which she had made possible by overcoming his misgivings, Ryan felt damn lucky. Which held fears of its own. Luck was hard to trust. He wasn't used to being loved for no other reason than love for its own sake.

His hands moved slowly along the back of her neck. "The water's warm. Want to swim?"

"If we get into the water, we'll scatter the stars," she smiled.

"Yeah." He unbuttoned his shirt and jeans and shed his clothes.

The sight of his naked body in moonlight was more than Emily could stand. She began to tremble. He slid the blouse from her shoulders and his lips moved over her skin and the flimsy barrier of lace.

As he kissed her shoulders and breasts, his hand found the buttons of her jeans. He urged her gently to her feet, knelt beside her and undressed her, caressing her legs. As the warmth of the summer night mingled with the heat of his hands, Emily felt wonderfully free.

Ryan wrapped her in his arms.

She admitted, "I've always wanted to swim naked in the moonlight."

They waded in together, into the sparkles and into the bright swath of light made by the moon, and allowed the water to caress their skin. Their bodies touched. Underwater caresses.

Emily couldn't breathe normally; her rising passion wouldn't let her. She wrapped her arms around him, moved her hands over him, felt his hands exploring her, felt his arousal.

They moved among the scattering stars, fireflies flashing all around them, until Ryan muttered, "I can't keep this up much longer..."

He carried her from the water out into the balmy air and lay her on the floating raft that swayed among the reeds. Lovingly he caressed her with his hands and his lips. The cool turned to fire and the flames threatened to consume her as his kisses became more intimate.

"Don't wait," she pleaded.

His wet body moved like a hot current over her. He looked down into her eyes and her name formed on his lips. She heard the mysterious music again.

His power and his heat and his strength rushed in. She shuddered with pleasure. Ryan moved with the rhythm of the music he didn't understand, rhythm of a love song sung to them by the spirits of the trees and flowers. Emily felt her body go so light it seemed to float away from her and into his and become a part of him. She gasped with pleasure. They were together... truly and completely... together...

Ryan's body went taut in the vortex of the music and he moaned and dropped against her, his heart beating hard, his heavy breaths very loud in the deep hush of night.

Her hands moved lovingly over his back, his hips, his thighs. She felt the scar.

Ryan rolled over and lay on his back on the raft, the moonlight bathing his body. "We didn't just scatter the stars," he said, out of breath. "We shattered them."

Emily turned toward the water where the quiet stars had returned. She said, "How fabulous to be shattered and then so quickly restored."

"It's all illusion," he said.

"What is?"

"Those stars," he mused, gazing at the sky. "Shattered and coming back together. Like us, tonight. It feels so chancy, Emily, like the least little ripple can make the whole surface shatter."

"And sparkle. Don't forget sparkle."

He closed his eyes, allowing her to pull him back out of the dark place he had sunk into, and smiled, still feeling the sensations of her love, and muttered, "I was dead wrong. What we've found together can't be a mistake." His hand gently caressed her shoulder. "No one else but you . . ."

"What?" she asked when he fell silent. "No one else but me what?"

"No one else could shatter stars," he said. "Or wear the moonlight in her hair."

It was nearly midnight when she left Wildwood. Sanders was waiting for her at the end of the driveway, as if he knew just what the plan was. Emily had tried to talk herself out of the absurd idea all evening; then she would remember Ralph's evil eyes. Her determination to stop him outweighed common sense.

The bright moonlight was both a help and hindrance. They could plainly see the target geese, but the chance of being seen was also greater. Emily drove with the lights off, pulled up in front of a house and produced the goose hat from her pocket to remind him the dog of their game. Sanders already knew. He leaped from the car door as she held it open, holding the light off, ran to the inert, white figure, grabbed the hat from its head and raced back. His reward was an enthusiastic pat and a gingerbread cookie, which he considered far superior to a dry old dog biscuit.

"Good boy! Now let's go get the next one!"

BEFORE SUNRISE, Ryan hovered at the edge of sleep, dreaming of stars. They fell from the sky and filled Emily's hair and formed a wedding veil. He held out his hand to welcome her into his life. But before she reached him, the stars turned to snow, a tumbling veil of white behind which the bride disappeared. Winter covered the landscape. The trees were stark and bare.

He woke slowly, unable to get out of the dream, easily interpreting its message: What Emily loved about Wildwood was the lush green summer. Theirs was, had always been, a summer love. Emily had called herself a gypsy. He had not seen any gypsy restlessness in her, but was it there, somewhere? Hidden? When deepest winter buried the landscape, could he trust her to stay?

Hell, he thought, it wouldn't work even if she did stay, with Craig in the picture. Craig wanted her and couldn't have her. Ryan cringed from the guilt of betraying his brother. He scratched his head and tried to make sense of it all . . . his guilt, his lack of trust, his hesitation to invite more pain on himself. There would be pain whatever he did. Last night in moonlight he had known he loved her. He had felt the explosion in his heart . . . unlike any sensations he had ever experienced. He'd known it was Emily Rose he wanted. And if he were ever to marry her, Craig would take it as betrayal. Could he live with that?

Could she? Would she ever be able to deal with the ghost nearby, now and always? Reality crawled over his mind like a deep ache. Eve Stark was going to marry that bum, and Emily would leave, unless he stopped her. Damn! He needed time and he didn't have it.

AT SIX-THIRTY in the morning Eve came running into Emily's room screaming, "My geese! Someone has stolen the bonnets off my geese!"

Emily struggled onto one elbow. Her eyes were barely open.

"Someone has stolen them!" Eve raved. "How could a person do such a thing?" She ran to answer the ringing telephone.

The shriek of her voice was enough to convey the neighborhood news that was coming in. Emily's eyes darted to the dresser, where the stolen goods were stashed. She had wanted to plant them in Ralph's truck outside his house last night, but the barking of his dogs had made it impossible.

Eve darted back into the sunny bedroom, her arms waving wildly. "A thief is loose! Goose hats are missing all around the neighborhood! People are in an uproar! It's the work of a sick mind."

"Probably so," Emily said, squinting in the sunlight. When she closed her eyes, she saw last night's stars floating around her and Ryan's beautiful body in the moonlight, but it was only a fleeting moment of bliss. Eve was pacing around her room saying the sheriff's office had already been called and Ralph was on his way over to comfort her.

These last remarks brought Emily to full attention. She threw off the sheet. "Okay, Aunt Eve, I'm up. I hope the coffee's on."

Anticipating Ralph's appearance in this hour of need, Eve hurried out to make more coffee. Emily dressed hurriedly and stuffed the tiny stolen goods into her pockets. This next was the most risky part; she herself would be exposed as the thief if she got caught. Brushing her hair, she heard the noisy pickup pull into the driveway. From the window, she watched Ralph get out of his truck, leaving the driver's door hanging open on its sprung hinges, as always. He would be heading for the kitchen where the food was, if she guessed right. With luck, she could slip out front unnoticed!

The air was filled with robins' songs and the brash cawing of crows, but there was no time to enjoy the magic of a summer morning. In a half crouch, Emily skulked along low bushes that lined the driveway, harassed by a scolding voice inside her that asked, *What am I doing?* She had been temporarily convinced that if the suggestion to frame Ralph came from a spirit, it would work, even though, by Craig's own admission, he wasn't using any special knowledge to come up with such a plan. The idea was just too dumb to work, and yet Craig had seemed so sure . . .

It was too late to turn back now, though; the truck was only a few yards away, and the door was standing wide open. She pulled the goods out of her pocket, darted for the truck, and with one quick stroke, stashed the goose hats under the driver's seat.

Two minutes later, she sauntered into the kitchen yawning. Ralph was seated there with a plate of toast in front of him and Eve was just hanging up the telephone.

"Who would have thought this could happen in our neighborhood?" she said. "I haven't had my goose garments threatened since those terrible Callister boys grew up. For all I know Ryan did it just to spite me. He hates me."

Emily had boosted herself up onto the counter and sat with her legs dangling over the dishwasher. She sputtered into her hot coffee. "Brilliant, Aunt Eve. The sheriff of Bluster County stealing hats off fake geese."

"You don't know him," Eve said.

From her place on the counter, Emily had a clear view of the driveway, through the wide window. She raised up as she caught a glimpse of Sanders running around out there, probably looking for her, maybe looking for his stolen treasures. And he would probably find them! She jumped down. "There's that shepherd dog again."

"It's the neighbor's dog," Eve said. "He's not supposed to be snooping around here. Ralph, run him off."

Emily followed him outside, on the run, yelling, "Don't be silly. He's perfectly friendly."

Huffing, Ralph raced out to the driveway waving his arms at the intruder. "Git! Git!"

The dog turned and looked at him. The wolf eyes narrowed. His mouth formed a snarl. Ralph's shouts stopped abruptly; he took several frightened steps back. Emily moved around and stood by the open door of the truck. The dog responded by loping toward his friend, ignoring the man. By now, Eve had picked up a broom and attempted to shoo the trespasser away; she shooed him right into the truck, or so it seemed. No one but Sanders had seen Emily's small signal. Before Ralph could express his outrage, the shepherd leaped out with a piece of bright fabric in his mouth. He set it in Emily's outstretched hand.

"Look at this!" she shouted, holding up a tiny red polka-dot hat.

Sanders, having done his duty and sensing trouble, trotted away, sniffing at the trees along the fence. No one saw him disappear. All three humans were staring at the little hat. Emily stuck her head into the truck. "There are more in here!" She brought out the small bundle. Aunt Eve's eyes were registering horror. Ralph was heading toward her at a fast clip. She handed the hats to Eve, glaring at Ralph. "I'm going in to call the sheriff! We've found the thief."

"Wait just a darn minute," Ralph said, turning his outrage on Emily. For an instant she saw the threat in his eyes and shivered with fear. *He knows,* she thought.

Eve stopped Ralph. "I saw this with my own eyes! How do you explain it?"

"Somebody else put them in my truck to make me look like a thief."

Emily ran up the front steps, and phoned in, leaving the message with the dispatcher at the sheriff's office. Her hands were trembling, as much out of anger at the threat in Ralph's eyes as the fear of her scheme somehow backfiring. She hurried back outside where Eve was going through the hats and Ralph was busy putting the blame on the dog.

"Don't act innocent, Ralph," Emily said. "You've been caught red-handed."

Eve's hands were fluttering wildly as if she were trying to erase a chalkboard. "This can't be! It simply can't be! There is some mistake."

"Damn right there is," Ralph gurgled. "What would I want with a bunch of doll hats?"

"That's true," Eve said.

The sheriff's car, which had been in the neighborhood, arrived, siren blaring. Emily was half disappointed, half relieved to see Deputy Beebe get out instead of Ryan. She handed him the evidence. "They were found in Mr. Peckham's truck," she said.

The deputy whipped out his tablet. "By who?"

"By the neighbor's dog."

"What neighbor would that be?"

"Sheriff Callister."

The deputy's eyebrows rose, then he took an authoritative stance with his hands on his hips. "I better read you your rights, mister."

"Don't be absurd," Eve wailed. "He's innocent! A motive is lacking."

"You got a motive?" the deputy asked his suspect.

"For snitching goose hats? What do you think?"

The deputy glared. "There's those that just enjoy making trouble. We got the tangible evidence, but I admit it don't make no sense." He turned and got into his car, saying, "I gotta call this in. Don't make no attempt to escape."

Eve was holding tightly, supportively, to her betrothed. Emily was feeling like an idiot. How could she have thought this stupid idea would work? It was her desperation to make Aunt Eve suspicious of Ralph, and she wasn't suspicious at all; she was standing by her man.

"Okay, I just talked to the sheriff and he says it's like this." Beebe hiked up his gun belt with both forearms.

"We'll cut a deal. You were found with stolen goods, which is automatic cause for arrest, and people are going to be pretty mad over this. Especially the victims. It's gonna make the paper—"

"No!" Eve wailed. "Not the paper!"

The lawman hushed her with his raised hand. "Or we can forget the arrest, nothing said and Peckham here can return every one of them little hats to the goose he stole it from."

Ralph's face turned crimson. "I won't do no such a thing!"

"Then I'm taking you in." He reached for his handcuffs.

An argument ensued, at the end of which, Ralph agreed to return the hats, with Eve's help, who knew where each probably belonged. Emily's scheme had backfired. She'd forgotten that women in love are blind.

"I was hoping he'd be arrested for his crime," she told Ryan later that night when she had crossed the meadow to meet him. "Why did you tell Beebe not to arrest him?"

"He'd have fought it with a lawyer," Ryan said. "And you could have ended up being implicated."

Her eyes widened in innocence. "Why me?"

"Because you're the one who did it. You and Sanders."

"How could you accuse us of such a vicious thing?"

"I'm a lawman, remember? I know the criminal mind."

She scowled. "You must be furious with me."

"If I didn't know Ralph's criminal history and your desperation, I'd be more furious. But when Beebe called in to say goose hats had been found in Peckham's truck, I broke up laughing. Hell, Emily, being a lawman in Bluster County, a guy has to have a sense of humor to survive."

Thank heaven he was being philosophical about this. "Crime doesn't pay, though," she said. "It only made matters worse. Ralph suspects me so he's pushing Eve harder. He took her to the village today and applied for a marriage license."

"That's how a con artist works," he said. "He's putting on a false personality, but the more time goes by the more likely he is to trip up someway. He has to strike before anything goes wrong, and now that he knows how far you'll go to stop him, he wants to get it done."

"Damn," she said, infuriated with herself. "I'd give anything if I could postpone that marriage long enough for Aunt Eve to come to her senses. She would, in time."

"I'm still working on it," Ryan said. "Believe me, Emily, I'm as determined to stop him as you are."

SATURDAY was market day in the village. From early morning, a group of Bluster County's good old boys gathered in the courthouse yard smoking and drinking. On this Saturday, Eve's wedding day, Ryan sauntered over from his office and joined them. He wasn't wearing his uniform.

The day before, he had seen two of the courthouse "regulars" talking with Ralph Peckham outside a local bar. Now, acting on a hunch, he was after information. An old-timer ceased his whittling and looked up. "Your leg bothering you bad this mornin', Sheriff?"

"Sure is," he answered truthfully.

"Sit yourself down then," offered Jed Muller, a farmer Ryan had known all his life. "Take a load off. Ain't you workin' today?"

"Just being sociable," Ryan answered, plopping down on a bench. He joined in the conversation, laughing at their jokes. After a time, when there was a lull, he smiled, "By the way, I'm aware that isn't cola in those cans. What've you guys got in there, beer or moonshine?"

Because drinking on the street of any town in Bluster County was illegal, he received no response and no one would look at him. Ryan grinned. "Never mind. I've got something else more important on my mind at the moment. Something I wanted to discuss with you boys. I've got a problem."

He leaned back against the side of the brick building and mused, "A mighty big problem. Some of you boys have been fishing at Wildwood for more years than I've been alive. I couldn't keep the fish population under control if it wasn't for you boys fishing the lake. Works out good for all of us. Things are about to change out there, though. A guy named Ralph Peckham—an outsider—is fixing to start a gun club next to my property. If that happens, there'll be no more peaceful afternoons at Wildwood. Strangers will be all over the place target shooting and taking boats out on the Stark end of the lake, ruining the fishing as well as the peace. I've spent my life on that land and I don't like it one damn bit."

"There's the biggest catfish in the county in your lake," the old-timer said.

"And the best ice fishin' there is," added another.

"Are you talking about the Stark farm?" another asked.

Ryan explained it to them, down to the details of the wedding and his own inability to legally put a stop to Ralph's plans, and finished with, "That club is gonna ruin it for all of us locals."

A groan resounded through the group. Looking at the men he'd seen talking to Peckham, both avid fishermen who fished at his lake regularly, Ryan continued, "This guy has no visible means of support and I've got some information that leads me to believe he moves right on the edge of the law." He made a point of eyeing the cola cans filled, illegally, with booze. "What I want is to stop that gun club. If any of you boys can help, I'll remember who did me the favor."

A long silence prevailed. Finally one man pulled his rimmed hat lower on his forehead and drawled, "Peckham's got a few acres in the hills. Ain't no road access in. I'm pretty dang sure he makes moonshine back there."

A man in bib overalls nodded. "He's got a still, all right. The rumor I heard was he started up an old still that's been back in them hills for years."

Ryan merely scratched his chin, showing no emotion. He'd suspected those two "friends" were after moonshine but without this admission, there was no proof. "Are there others in it with him?"

"One or two maybe. And they might be at the site and armed."

Ryan got to his feet. "I consider this conversation strictly confidential, boys. And I thank you." He nodded a farewell and headed for the courthouse steps.

"Take care of that leg, Sheriff," one man called.

He knew he was favoring the leg more than usual, and wondered how many of the townspeople were aware of the fact that he'd been putting off surgery. Everything that was his business got all over town, especially among the unmarried young women, who kept close tabs on his personal life. The pain in his leg was of real concern to him right now because he was envisioning heading out to climb some hills.

It took only a few minutes to locate Ralph's land on a plat at the county surveyor's office. Ryan knew the area of dense forested hills not far from Appleyard Farm. In earlier decades there were stills all through those thick woods, and it was common knowledge that some existed yet. Finding them at random was impossible, but he could narrow this one down to a three-mile radius, and if the still was presently in operation, there had to be some footpaths leading in.

His watch read nine o'clock. He had to hurry if he was going to get his evidence in time to try to stop the wedding. Back in his office, he phoned Emily and told her where the still was located, above Ralph's roadside property in the wild hills where there were no roads and few trails. It wasn't far away as the crow flies, he said, but a challenge to get to on foot.

"Can you make it?" Emily asked, elated at the news but worried at the same time. "Are you taking Beebe with you?"

"Beebe refuses—he's afraid of snakes," Ryan said dryly. "Sanders is more help, anyway. He can sniff out the still. I'll try to get back by two-thirty at the latest."

Her heart fluttered with fear. "What if you don't?"

"Then you'll just have to stall."

"Stall . . . ?"

"Got to hurry," he said. "I love you."

The words rang in her ear like musical chimes. He had hung up before she caught her breath to answer.

EMILY couldn't shake a frightening feeling that something was going to go wrong. Soon after talking to Ryan, she took the raft over to Pillywiggin to fill Craig in on the tense situation.

Craig was waiting in the shadows. She had seen him only once since the goose-hat fiasco. He'd been a little subdued after learning how his suggestions had backfired, and had expressed his desire to somehow make it up to her.

"Ryan found out Peckham has a still in the hills," she told him. "He's gone up there to find it. I'm so worried! Sometimes men guard stills with guns. Ryan could get himself killed."

"Why didn't he wait for reinforcement?" Craig wanted to know.

"Because there wasn't time. The wedding is today. He has to find the evidence so he can put Ralph under arrest *before* the wedding. He's only got until three o'clock. And if he doesn't find it and get back by two-thirty, he said to stall. How can I, though, Craig? How can I stall a wedding?"

"Pretend to get lost on the way to the church, maybe?"

"I'm not driving Aunt Eve. Ralph insists on picking her up to take her to the church. He probably thinks I'll kidnap her and run. He'll be at the farm at two-thirty and if Ryan isn't back by then to arrest him for operating the still, it'll be too late!"

"No. We'll stall. I'll just have to take Ryan's place if he doesn't get back," he said. "I've been practicing materializing. I think I can pull it off at the farm."

Her mouth fell open. "Pretend to be Ryan? Can you?"

He grinned. "Don't worry, Emily. You can count on me. But I'm going to leave you now, to preserve my energy. That's only a few hours away. It'll take all my concentration."

Before her eyes, he faded and was gone. But his voice came echoing through. "See ya."

It ought to work; if Craig had fooled her, he could fool Ralph. But the more she thought about it, the more nervous she became. Craig seemed to have a rather ungrounded perspective on things. And he wasn't the one who had to pay the consequences if his flighty schemes misfired.

11

AT TWO TWENTY-FIVE Emily was dressed for the wedding. She and Lucille Post were helping the bride with her hair in an upstairs bedroom when they heard Ralph's pickup pull into the driveway. Emily began to panic. Ryan wasn't back yet. Would Craig really go through with his wild scheme? And if he did successfully impersonate Ryan, what would happen if Ryan were to drive up at the same time?

She rushed to the window. Ralph was turning the red pickup around in the driveway so the passenger side would face the front of the house, ready for his bride to enter. Emily's heart began to pound. She watched from above as Ralph dawdled, stretching up to the mirror to adjust his bow tie. Seconds later a blurry figure appeared out of nowhere at the driver's window. She gazed wide-eyed as his head and shoulders came into focus before her eyes. Craig had done it!

He hadn't driven up, of course, as Ryan would, or even walked up, for that matter. And he was wearing the T-shirt he always wore, not a sheriff's uniform. She cringed. He probably wasn't even wearing shoes; from this angle, she could see only his head and shirt, but that was all Ralph would be able to see, from inside the truck.

Ralph turned from the mirror and jumped, startled, to see the sheriff of Bluster County.

Through the open window she heard Ralph begin to curse. His words were indecipherable, but Emily knew he was threatened by the appearance of the lawman. She could only guess what Craig was saying.

"What's happening?" Lucille asked, fussing with a flower for the bride's hair. She joined Emily at the window. "Who is that talking to Ralph?"

"It looks like the...uh...sheriff," Emily replied meekly.

"Sheriff? Are you sure? I don't see his car."

Eve found a place at the window, between them. She looked down on the scene, sputtering, "Yes, that's the sheriff, all right."

The feeling of disaster that had plagued Emily all morning, rushed over her like an electric current. "I'll go see what the deal is," she said, already out of the bedroom door before the sentence was finished. She rushed down the stairs and out the front entry, ran around to the opposite side of the truck, to back up Craig's impersonation efforts, and stopped dead.

From the waist up, Craig looked as he always did, but his efforts to totally materialize had failed. He had no legs! She felt suddenly faint.

"You're under arrest for operating an illegal still," Craig was saying gruffly, without benefit of a gun. "Get out of the truck."

"No!" Emily protested from behind him. "No! Don't get out—!"

They were too involved in their ensuing confrontation to pay attention. "You ain't takin' me in!" Ralph was growling as he pushed open the door, ready for a fight.

The door should have slammed into the sheriff's chest, but there was no sound from the hit. Emily glanced up at the window, terrified that Eve and Lucille were on their way down where they would see that "Ryan" was trying to arrest Ralph without benefit of legs. But, hesitant to have the groom see her before she was ready, Eve remained at the window. Emily prayed Craig would stay behind the truck.

Ralph wasn't waiting for the officer to get the jump on him. He barely touched ground before he lunged. His punch connected with nothing but air. Thrown off-balance, struggling for a firm stance, he made a grab for the truck door for support. It was then he saw his accuser.

His face went wild with terror. He began screaming like a banshee and took off running through the meadow. His screams became less piercing as he put distance between himself and the object of his terror.

"What a chicken," Craig said, shaking his head. "I knew people were scared of Ryan, but I never saw anything to equal this."

"Don't move!" Emily warned. "Whatever you do, don't move! Stay behind the truck!" Her gaze moved to the upper window again where women were watching the dark-suited groom tearing across the meadow, giving no indication that he was ever going to stop.

"Hey, it worked, didn't it?" Craig asked. "What's wrong?"

"Look down," she said in a hoarse whisper. "You don't have any legs! That's what scared him."

"Hell, you're right. I've been gone so long I tend to forget details."

"You mean like a gun if you're going to arrest somebody? Or a uniform? Or a means of transportation, maybe? Or *legs?*"

He laughed. "Ralph's gone, though, that's the thing."

"I don't think he's gone for long, no matter how scared he is. In fact, I know he'll be back. He's too determined to get this wedding done...." She sucked in her breath. "Craig, you're fading!"

"I can't keep the illusion," he said. "It's too hard. I've got to go, Emily."

When she turned, Aunt Eve and Lucille were running toward her from the house. Eve was yelling, "Where is he? I saw Ryan Callister! He must have threatened Ralph with a gun! Threatened to shoot him! Poor Ralph! Running for his life!" She looked around. "Where'd the sheriff go so fast? Where is he?"

Where is he? the voice in Emily's head echoed in panic. Unless something were wrong, he'd be here by now. That awful feeling nagged and prickled and wouldn't leave.

Craig had done all he could, and once again, his plan might easily have caused a disaster. It was up to her now, and time was running out.

RYAN must be in trouble! People got lost in these woods all the time, Emily knew, but Sanders was with him. The dog wouldn't get lost. Ryan might have been discovered by one of Ralph's cronies guarding the site, but that wasn't likely, either; Ryan was an expert at his job. It was his leg she was worried about; it had been bothering him, and the climb would be grueling. Ryan had given her his location for a reason. He'd have figured somebody besides the incompetent Beebe needed to know he was heading back into the hills.

Aunt Eve would assume she was going to look for Ralph. She waved at Eve and Lucille and hurried to her car.

It was easy to find the spot where Ryan had gone into the woods back of Ralph's property; his sheriff's car was parked by the fence.

Barbed wire ripped her dress when she climbed through, and as she began to walk, the forest became more dense and dark. What she thought had been a deer path disappeared. She had no idea which way to go. This was crazy! What chance would she possibly have of finding Ryan in here? If she got herself lost it would make matters worse. Frightened and discouraged, she called out his name.

The wooded hills were eerily silent. Emily took a few more unsure steps between the moss-grown trees, and called again, ducking from the echo of her voice. Some moments later Sanders came bounding out of the forest. The dog had heard her call!

For once Sanders didn't rush up to be petted. He barked once and trotted a short distance back up through the trees before he turned around to make sure she was following.

"I'm coming!" she called, already out of breath.

Sanders led the way. It wasn't a long climb before they reached Ryan, who was collapsed on the ground, holding his leg, his face covered with perspiration.

Sanders ran up and began licking his forehead. Ryan raised his head. "Emily! I can't believe it!"

"I was so worried! Are you all right?"

"No, hell no. My leg is killing me. I twisted it so hard on the climb I just couldn't go any farther." He patted Sanders head, acknowledging his gratitude. "Damn! The wedding will be—"

"The wedding will be starting late," she said, interrupting him. "How badly are you hurt?"

"Pretty bad. I can feel something really wrong and the pain won't let up."

She fought back tears. "How can I help? Can you lean on me?"

"Maybe. I'm a lot heavier than you, but if I support part of my weight on a stick, maybe I can make it." He struggled to get to his feet, muttering, "I've got the evidence to arrest Ralph, including Polaroid photos of the still."

"Oh, Ryan, thank God!" Emily drew an arm around his waist and allowed him to lean on her shoulder. He moaned in pain when he put weight on the leg. "I can hold more weight," she insisted. "Don't be afraid to lean on me. I'll go as slow as you say."

Sanders led them the short distance down. It was slow going, but Ryan forced himself to keep walking. At the bottom, where thigh-high grass replaced the trees, he managed to get through the fence, but once in the car, breathing heavily, he hesitated. "Will you drive?"

"No problem." She got in behind the wheel and pulled away, leaving her own car parked beside the fence.

"Wow, this thing has power!"

Ryan only moaned. "Will they still be at the house?"

"I doubt if they've left for the church without me. They think I'm looking for Ralph."

"Looking for him?"

She kept her eyes on the road, driving fast. "There isn't time to explain it, Ryan. We'll be there in a couple of minutes."

"Oh, brother." He leaned back against the headrest and closed his eyes. "After the goose hats trick, I'm not sure I want to know."

Another minute at this speed brought them to Appleyard Farm. "They haven't left yet," she told Ryan. "But it looks like we just made it."

He opened his eyes and sat up. As they pulled in, Ralph was standing in the driveway by Eve's car. The bride and her friend were on the front porch gathering up their bouquets.

All heads turned toward the sheriff's car squealing into the driveway, Emily at the wheel. Ryan pulled out his gun and got out when the car jerked to a stop. He walked toward Ralph, his face covered with perspiration, limping badly, his gun drawn. Ralph's eyes were fixed on his visible legs.

Emily stepped out in her torn dress.

"What's happening?" Eve cried, running down the front steps. "Emily, why are you driving the sheriff's car? Where on earth have you been?"

Ryan's eyes were studying Ralph's. He knew Ralph had noted the way he was limping and the way he was now supporting himself on the car. He could also tell by the way he swayed that his suspect had been drinking. "Don't try anything, Peckham. You're under arrest."

"You're nuts, Sheriff! I ain't done nothin'!"

"For illegal distilling of whiskey."

Ralph's eyes grew wild. "I already told you once, you ain't takin' me in!" Because Ryan was obviously hurt and at a disadvantage, Peckham rushed forward, trying to hit his right leg and the arm that held the gun. Ryan stepped back. Ralph tumbled forward and began to fight, his arms flailing in all directions.

Emily, knowing how much pain Ryan was in, was ready to lunge at Ralph, but her help wasn't needed. In pain or not, the sheriff was a strong man and experienced in defending himself. He grabbed the criminal by the lapels of his coat, swung him around, and with his free hand reached for the handcuffs in his back pocket.

Ralph was subdued, all but his mouth. "This is about my gun club, ain't it? Listen to me, Sheriff, I'll cut you in. There's big money to be made. We'll be partners, you and me . . ."

"You're under arrest for operating a still," Ryan growled, breathing hard. He began reciting Peckham his rights.

Peckham was desperate. "I gotta get to the church! Sheriff, listen! It's gonna be my land! I'll cut you in . . ."

By this time Eve and Lucille were standing behind Ralph, hearing every word. When Eve cried out his name, her groom-to-be turned toward her, his breath reeking.

"You're drunk! Ralph! And I heard what you said . . ." She burst into tears.

"Operating a still!" Lucille gasped, looking across at Emily. "Is it true?"

Emily nodded, hurrying to Eve's side. She circled her arms around her. Eve sobbed, "Ralph makes ... moonshine? He's been drinking it, too! Ralph is drunk, Emily!"

"He's not the man you thought he was," Emily said, watching Ryan guide his handcuffed prisoner roughly into the back seat.

Eve broke away from her and marched to the car as if she were a soldier on patrol. She poked her face into the back seat, then brought it out again, waving her hand. "You reek of whiskey!"

"You don't understand, darlin'," Ralph began. "The sheriff ... he didn't have no legs ..."

Eve squinted and snarled with disgust. "Is it true about the still?"

"Not a word!"

Ryan, standing beside her, waiting for Emily, said, "It's an open-and-shut case, Mrs. Stark. The still and his possessions are up there in the woods not four miles from here. I regret you had to find out this way."

Eve stared up into the sky blue eyes of the startlingly handsome young man who had spoken to her with such a gentle voice. Emily saw her aunt look at Ryan Callister as if she were seeing him for the first time. Not as a boy. Or even as a sheriff. But as a man, with feelings.

"My Eve will put up bail," Ralph yelled. "I'll still make my wedding and no one can stop me."

"*I* can stop you!" It was Eve, her voice shaking with anger. "I heard what you said about my farm, you drunken sot! Oh, how could I have been so fooled!"

Emily straightened with pride. Aunt Eve wasn't the mouse she'd feared she was. With Leo gone, Eve hadn't forgotten she was free. She was her own woman.

Lucille pranced up to get in her two cents, calling Ralph an "inebriated fungus." She urged her friend away from the window. Ralph had begun to struggle, resisting the handcuffs and swearing at Ryan.

Ryan hadn't gotten in the car. He and Emily exchanged glances. "I've got to go, Aunt Eve," she said. "Ryan's leg is hurting him so badly it isn't safe to drive."

"It's illegal for anyone except an officer of the law to drive the sheriff's car," Ryan said when she reached him.

"But you can't! It's dangerous, especially with a struggling prisoner in the back." She frowned at him and whispered, "From the way you look, Ryan, you could pass out any minute."

"I might. I'm hurting bad." He leaned on the car for support, wincing. "I'll just have to deputize you. Do you swear to uphold the law?"

Her eyes grew wide. "Deputize? Uh...uphold... yes..."

"Consider yourself deputized," he said.

"Is that all there is to it?"

"No, but if anyone asks, you're a deputy sheriff. I'd prefer you didn't try to make an arrest, though." He opened the passenger door and slid onto the seat.

Lucille's mouth had dropped open, watching them. "Eve! Do you see this? Your niece and Sheriff Callister?"

Emily hurried around to the driver's side, calling out, "I'll explain later, Aunt Eve."

Ryan radioed his office that they were bringing a prisoner in. During the fourteen-minute drive, with Ralph behind them making threats of everything from suing Emily to hinting of murder, they said nothing, either to him or to each other. Ryan was busy writing on a clipboard.

They were met by Deputy Beebe, who, blustering with importance, took charge of leading the prisoner into the jail. Ryan handed him the clipboard and Polaroid shots without getting out of the car, and asked Emily to drive around the corner to the doctor's office.

She parked in the emergency space. Ryan was willing to lean on her while he hobbled in. She knew he had about reached the end of his pain tolerance. When the alarmed receptionist saw them, she held open the door of the inner office and motioned them inside to an examining room. The doctor entered right behind them, blocking the doorway so Emily couldn't quickly leave.

"Well, Ryan, I can't say I'm surprised to see you," he said. "I've been warning you about that leg. Let's have a look."

Ryan began unbuttoning his jeans, saying, "By the way, this is Emily Rose. Doc Morgan."

She nodded and quickly scooted out the door. Eight minutes later, a nurse appeared in the waiting room to summon her back inside.

Ryan was dressed, still sitting on the examining table. "I have to get to the hospital," he said.

"That's the hospital in Waddleville," the doctor explained. "There's a bullet fragment still in that leg that shifted when he twisted it. This leg needs X rays and immediate attention. He can't put off surgery any longer."

"Mind driving me, Deputy Rose?" Ryan asked. "I've just had a shot of a painkiller that's making me dizzy."

"The drug is going to make him very drowsy," Dr. Morgan confirmed.

"Of course I'll drive," Emily offered, only now remembering that her own car was still parked in a back field. By calling her Deputy Rose, Ryan meant they'd be taking the sheriff's car, the only one available.

By the time they were on the road, Ryan was so drowsy he could barely talk. Emily was relieved to see the pain medication work, but she was uneasy about driving an official car with a sleeping sheriff beside her. What would people think? Trying to be less conspicuous, she set Ryan's uniform hat, which he rarely wore and kept on the car seat, over her blond hair. What if they encountered some sheriff-type emergency on the way?

Any ideas she might have had about making fast time in a marked car turned out to be false hope; the opposite was true. Cars in front of them and behind them slowed down.

"Stupid people . . ." she muttered in frustration.

"Huh?"

She turned. He was perspiring again. "Ryan, are you doing okay?"

He shifted around with discomfort. "Can you get there any faster?"

"Not with everybody slowing to a crawl around us. "There's almost a traffic jam." She glanced at him again. He looked awful. Was the medication beginning to wear off already?"

"Okay, I'll go faster," she muttered, reaching for the switches on the panel. In seconds the siren began to wail and a red light was flashing on the top of the car. It worked like magic! All vehicles in front began pulling over to the side. Emily pressed down hard on the gas pedal and felt the imposing power of the engine kick in. She hunched behind the wheel, her pulse pumping wildly, and raced down the cleared highway at such an awesome speed her knuckles were white on the wheel.

Ryan stirred in the passenger seat and opened his eyes. "What the *hell?*"

"Now we're making time!" she said, her eyes fixed on the whir of pavement in front of them.

When they had reached the emergency room doors and Ryan was wheeled in, Emily was left in the small waiting room just outside. She paced nervously for several minutes until a volunteer in a pink uniform directed her to a coffee machine. The warmth in her stomach helped her trembling, but didn't stop her mind from racing. Not until she finally sat down did she realize the sheriff's hat was still on her head.

The wild events of the day replayed in her mind: Craig's failed attempt at impersonating Ryan. The sight of Ryan as she came through the trees on the hill. The fright of Ralph's challenge and Ryan's reaction—his ability to protect himself while subduing a criminal, even when he could barely walk. The ease with which he could take another man into custody. His willingness to ask for her help. Was it because she was his lover and he trusted her? Wanted her with him? Or was it because he was in too much pain to consider alternatives on the spur of the moment?

A telephone on the wall reminded her that poor Aunt Eve was going through a hell of her own.

"I had to call collect because I don't have my purse," Emily said. "I'm still with Ryan Callister. He's at the Waddleville hospital. Ralph is in the county jail. Are you okay, Aunt Eve?"

Her voice was surprisingly calm. "Yes, dear. My friends are with me. We're having lemonade and cookies. I'm so thankful I found out about Ralph in time. I shudder to think. You knew he was no good, didn't you? And everything you tried to tell me just went in both ears and out the other end."

Eve's metaphors. Emily grinned. "Ralph married for money twice before, Aunt Eve, and divorced his wives after he lost everything they had."

A gasp sounded through the phone. "How do you know this?"

"Ryan found out. But we knew you wouldn't listen to him."

"He? We? Emily, have you been—?"

"We've been friends since I visited ten years ago."

"I can't believe it! When I saw..." She stumbled over the words. "What was wrong with him today? He was hurt. Is that why you're at the hospital?"

"Yes. He has to have surgery on his leg. Where Uncle Leo shot him. The leg never healed."

"Oh my!" Eve sounded suddenly very upset. "You mean that's why he . . ." She stopped.

"That's why he limps. Surely you knew that."

"No . . . no. Leo told me he limped because he broke his leg falling out of a tree."

"Leo lied. You know, Aunt Eve, if you didn't forbid anyone from talking about the Callisters, you'd know a lot of things about him. Like the fact that he's always been really nice to me." Emily knew she could say it now because Ryan had saved Aunt Eve today at no little risk to himself and Eve couldn't help but know it.

"We must talk, Emily. When will you be home?"

"I don't know. I'm waiting to find out if I can see Ryan. If I'm late, don't worry."

IT WAS HOURS before the nurse finally summoned her. "Mr. Callister has been taken to room 204."

Legs trembling, carrying Ryan's hat, she hurried up the stairs. The door to room 204 was open.

He was lying propped against a pillow, his eyes closed, covered to the waist with a blanket. Emily moved closer on tiptoe to keep her heels from clicking on the tile floor. He looked pale. In the light from half-closed blinds at the window, she could see the shadows of his eyelashes. His face stunned her, even now, in drug-induced sleep. How beautiful he was! How wide his shoulders looked in the white, loose-fitting gown. She stood over him for a full minute before his eyes fluttered open as if he felt a presence. "Emily?"

She leaned closer. "I thought you were asleep. Knocked out."

"I'm awake."

"Is the pain better?"

"With the drugs, yeah."

"When are they going to operate?"

"I don't know. A surgeon is coming from Blooming-ton in the morning to examine my leg." He sighed. "Thanks for waiting so long. They were doing tests."

"I didn't mind. But I was worried."

He smiled weakly. "About me? Hell, if I could survive the ride over here I can survive anything."

His voice was not as strong as usual, and he seemed distracted, concerned about something. She wondered what the doctors had told him.

But it wasn't his immediate medical prognosis that was bothering Ryan at the moment. He said, "When I was half dozing in the car, I got to wondering how you managed to stall the wedding and why Peckham was drunk. I got a sinking feeling about that scheme you weren't anxious to confess to this afternoon."

She wrung her hands. "I didn't know what to do, Ryan. You had said to stall the wedding if you didn't get back by two-thirty, and I didn't know how. So Craig...Craig had this idea about impersonating you...to Ralph...he thought he could do it..."

Ryan closed his eyes. His jaw muscles stiffened. "Go on."

"Well, he pretty much flubbed it. I mean, showing up just out of the blue with no warning and...and...he did look just like you only—" she winced "—only he hadn't had enough practice and he didn't manage to materialize his whole body. Below the waist he was invisible. One glance and Ralph took off running like he'd been shot out of a cannon. That's why he was drunk when we got there. Obviously he needed something to get up the courage to come back. He thought it was you...without legs."

Ryan raised his arm over his eyes and lay very still. She watched his chest rise and fall, heard his breathing, which was heavier than it had been.

When she couldn't stand the silence any longer, she said, "I know it was a stupid plan but it turned out okay because it goaded Ralph into getting drunk. Which was the last straw for Aunt Eve."

After another agonizing silence, he said finally, his arm still covering his eyes, "So you've been seeing Craig on the island, then, and making it a point not to tell me."

She winced at how deceitful this sounded. "He was afraid you'd be mad. Jealous, maybe."

"Jealous of a ghost?" He moved his arm and looked up at her. "Is that what you thought?"

"Well, I . . . guess so . . . he told me. Maybe I even thought it was the other way around—that he'd be jealous of you. I mean, he told me how he loved me so much and didn't think it was fair that you had such an advantage."

Ryan stared in amazement. "I don't think I'm hearing this right. What reason could you have for conspiring with him, Emily, behind my back? I just don't get it."

"I feel sorry for him, Ryan!"

He was silent.

"Don't you?" she asked softly.

He wet his dry lips. "I don't know what I feel. But I know as long as Craig is around, you and I don't have a chance. If he were alive, I'd fight him over this. But he's dead, and I . . . it's hard to ignore his feelings about you. I had no idea you had feelings for him as well. I mean, after you knew he wasn't me. Maybe I should have guessed, though. It was Craig you had the midnight date with and Craig you thought about for ten years. I shouldn't have let you think otherwise. I wasn't trying to be deceitful. I just wasn't ready to explain about my brother when we were standing there on the street that first day."

She didn't like the way Ryan was talking, nor the fact that he so completely misunderstood. She deeply regretted letting Craig talk her into the secrecy against her better judgment. "Ryan, I met Craig on the island to confront him about the two of you tricking me, and when I found out he was . . . a ghost and wanted my friendship, I could see nothing wrong with it. I should have told you."

"Exactly what did you think I'd do if I knew?"

"Maybe what you're doing now. Acting upset."

He looked up at her, his eyes filled with sadness, and said, "We'll never be free of this, Emily. With Craig in the picture, it'll never work. I'll feel guilty all the time and you'll be torn both ways."

"I'm not torn, Ryan! I mean, I want to be his friend, but you and I are much more than that."

He closed his eyes again. "He has enough of a hold on you to talk you into deceiving me. And he always will. I know him better than you."

The conversation was making her feel ill. She wanted to cut it off, for Ryan's sake, because he was full of pain medication and groggy and feeling awful. But it had to be finished and they both knew it. She reasoned, "You sound so bitter, Ryan. But you love him."

He nodded. "When Craig died I lost the person I loved most in life. Don't you see, Emily? It's because I love him that I can't just shove him aside and live as though he weren't here? When he is here. And you can't, either."

Tears filled her eyes and spilled down her cheeks. "You're right. We'd never have any...real peace, would we? No matter how much we tried?"

"No." He paused for a long time, breathing faster. "And winter will come—" He stopped.

She waited. "Winter? What does winter have to do with it?"

"The deep winter is bleak. Cold. You and your gypsy blood wouldn't like the winters in the country."

A pain stabbed through her. She felt as though something had just been torn out of her. "You're asking me not to stay, aren't you, Ryan?"

He looked at her dazedly. It was impossible to determine whether it was the drug or his emotions affecting his eyes. Or both. He muttered, "I don't know any way to make it work for us without fighting Craig. Right now I don't know how to do that."

She was silent.

"Do you?" he asked.

She shook her head. What he said was true. Craig did have some strange hold on her, and on his twin as well, and as long as he could talk to either of them, she and Ryan could never really be alone.

Ryan reached for her hand. "There's no need for you to stick around the hospital. In fact, please don't. I'm dreading the surgery and I'm going to be feeling damn awful for the next few days and I'm lousy company when I'm sick."

She tried to control her tears. "Are you sure?"

"Yeah."

"Then if that's what you want . . . I'll just wish you luck." What a horrible way for their beautiful romance to end. With an aching heart, she bent down and kissed his forehead. "See ya, Ryan."

"See ya," he said without opening his eyes.

It was raining when she left the hospital and drove home in the sheriff's car, praying no one would stop her for any reason. It would be bad enough trying to explain having no driver's license and no proof she was a sheriff's deputy. The tears that blurred her vision, like the rain, would be even harder to explain.

RYAN TRIED to turn over, but restraints on his leg stopped him. He felt as if he were choking, but the pain wasn't in his throat; it was in his heart. Never had he felt so alone, now that he had pushed Emily away, and never had he needed anyone or wanted anyone the way he wanted her.

Trouble was, he could barely think, with the discomfort and the medication and the dread of tomorrow. And the voice of his brother close . . . too close.

He didn't hear the nurse approach, and jumped when she touched him. She bent down to him, concerned over the tear that spilled when he opened his eyes.

"Is there something I can do for you?" she asked.

"Just leave me alone."

He closed his burning eyes and turned his head away.

12

AFTER LAST NIGHT'S RAIN, the morning was foggy. Water dripped from the trees, splashing on the lawn and the flowers. The sun burst through and the world began to sparkle.

Emily thought of Ryan waking in the hospital. Would he have surgery today? It was possible, but not certain. She ought to be at his side, making this easier for him, but he didn't want her there. More evidence that Ryan was basically a loner, and that he had never learned to cope with the loss of the one person he'd been closest to. Identical twins had a special bond, not easily broken, even by death.

What Craig was doing was unfair to Ryan; she should have seen it sooner. Yet Craig had wanted to help Ryan. He did care about him, probably very deeply. Maybe he could be reasoned with.

Thinking about swimming over to Pillywiggin this morning, Emily was still in bed when Aunt Eve knocked on her door and came in. The sight of her brought Emily to attention. She went suddenly stiff with fear.

"Aunt Eve! Why are you wearing your wedding dress?"

"It's Sunday, dear. I've decided to wear it to church. I refuse to let this lovely dress gather dust in the closet. Besides, everybody will be staring at me today so I might as well look my best."

"That's a smashing idea." Emily studied her carefully for signs of strain. The news of Ralph's arrest would be all over this part of the county by now. "Is it going to be awful for you, Aunt Eve?"

She shook her head. "No. I have a bag of my own tricks so I pulled a rabbit out from under the rug. After you told me about Ralph's background, Lucille and I spread the word that I had found out and that I had a hand in the entire investigation and the wedding was just part of the sting operation."

"Sting operation?" Aunt Eve watched too much TV.

"It's a white lie, I know. But sometimes white lies can serve us well. Success is the mother of invention."

Emily smiled. "So you'll be the local heroine today."

"Yes, I'll be the center of attention. I thought of wearing a flower in my hair and then decided it might be too much. Don't you think? You're going with me, aren't you, dear? You'll be at my side?"

"Of course I will." She threw off the sheet, knowing it must be getting late. Pillywiggin would have to wait; besides, Craig wasn't going anywhere.

"I'll make some fresh coffee." Aunt Eve stopped to admire herself in the mirror. She did look lovely in blue, with her silver hair and rose-toned skin. "You were right, Emily, I was rushing things. I do look nice for a woman my age, don't I?"

"You're beautiful," Emily said, meaning it.

"There are lots of fish in the sea. Better than Ralph. Fish who don't lie." She smiled, turning again at the mirror. "I'm going to wear a pretty dress to church every Sunday from now on."

IT WAS APPROACHING midafternoon when Aunt Eve lay down for a nap, exhausted from the excitement of the circle of well-wishers at an after-church social hour. Emily changed quickly into her swimsuit and a shift and her canvass shoes, and made her way along the shore to the cove behind Pillywiggin Island. She was joined by Sanders, who ran with her for a time and then, distracted by the scent of another dog, disappeared into the high grass.

The afternoon was warm and smelled of honeysuckle. Small water lilies were in full bloom on the lake. It was hard to appreciate the beauty when her heart felt so empty. Ryan might as well have been across the world; such was the barrier between them.

The warm water felt soothing around her as she swam to the tiny beach. She ducked under the bramble as she had so many times before, and called Craig's name. He didn't appear at once, but as she began to walk toward the swings, he was suddenly there.

"Hi, Emily."

Did she imagine it or was his voice a little different today? "Hi," she answered, and sat down in the swing. The ghost sat in the other swing and they began to move in the same rhythm. "Ralph is in jail," she said. "And the wedding is off."

He smiled. "Good."

"Ryan is in the hospital. He had a rough day with that leg. He barely made it down the hill and then Peckham put up a fight, resisting arrest. It didn't take Ryan long to subdue him but it hurt his leg even more."

"I know."

For a time silence washed over the little island. Craig was more quiet than usual, and Emily was trying to think of the best way to approach the subject that was on her mind. Certainly she liked to be with him because he was always so carefree and fun. But he wasn't human now; he was illusion. Like her gypsy dreams.

"Ryan found out I've been meeting you here," she said softly. "He was pretty mad. He said it was deceitful."

"I guess technically, it was," Craig admitted. "I didn't see why he'd have to know, though."

She took a deep breath and began cautiously, "I should have told him. We both should have. The thing is, Craig, I like you very much...you know that. In fact, I love you. I love you as a spirit. But I love Ryan as a man. And it's not the same."

His swing moved with no apparent effort from him. He seemed to be considering this deeply. "I thought it *was* me you loved, though. I mean before."

"Before?"

"Ever since we were kids, all the time in between. Like I loved you."

"I loved a boy I didn't really know. Who, it turns out, was really two boys. There were such wonderful memories, you know. It's not easy to forget the magic of a first kiss."

He fell into silence. She sat very still, caught in dread. "What's wrong?"

"I've never kissed you," Craig said softly.

Emily let this sink in, trying to hide the soft, warm sensations that filled her heart. It had been Ryan all along. For a long time, neither spoke. Finally she understood she had to pull them back to reality, whatever that was.

She said, "It isn't just a rivalry like in the past, Craig. This is different. You can't compete with Ryan anymore, and he can't . . . he can't take advantage of that fact without hurting you. He doesn't want to hurt you, so he . . ."

"He hurts himself instead." Craig finished the sentence. His voice softened. "Yeah, I know. I see that now."

She felt a deep, very real ache. "It hurts me, too, Craig. Don't you see? Ryan loves you too much for his own good. Maybe I do, too. There are three of us who love each other but only two who are alive. . . ."

Craig fell into another silence, this one so profound that Emily reeled from the fear that her words had hurt him very badly.

When he spoke, it was not what she had expected. "My brother is alone," he said. "I didn't want that. I didn't realize . . . what I'd done."

She turned with questioning eyes. "What do you mean?"

"Last night. I was there. I didn't know I could manage to be with him—you know—guarding over him, but yesterday when he was hurting so much, hurting more inside than from that leg, I was able to find him easily. I tried to comfort him without his knowing, but there wasn't anything I could do because I was the cause. I didn't understand until then. I'm a slow learner. I didn't realize we couldn't keep playing the old games anymore. But when I saw him in that hospital room, so alone...I couldn't stand it. I felt his sadness all through me." He looked at her through a glaze of silver. "He wanted you there, Emily."

Her eyes filled with tears.

"And you wanted to be there."

"More than anything," she admitted, and paused, hearing a noise. The nearby bushes rustled.

Ryan stepped into the clearing, wearing the same clothes as yesterday, jeans and a blue short-sleeved shirt that reflected the color of his eyes, and he had a day's growth of beard. Emily blinked, as if he, too, were an apparition.

"Hey, buddy," Craig said. "What'd you do, escape the institution?"

Ryan didn't answer. He stood just outside the thicket, staring at an image of himself, real and illusory, as if it were a reflection in a mirror. He could no longer look into a mirror without seeing, not himself, but his twin. It was like that now—that same blood-stirring sensation—in this silent clearing. Craig stood before him in a slant of light, but there was no mirror here, and no distant reach of time. He looked as he had seen him last, in jeans and a dark T-shirt, his easy smile unchanged. Only his eyes were different, no longer blue, but faded to silver.

"Craig?" The voice was barely audible, the pain in his leg forgotten, the pain in his heart put momentarily on hold. Something in his whirling mind pulled out his brother's earlier words . . . he could materialize if he wanted to . . .

Emily shivered and stepped back into the shadows; she would not stand between them.

"It's you . . ." Ryan uttered, as elation and confusion clashed in his head like free waves bouncing off a rock cliff.

Craig replied with a smile. "Illusion. Just illusion. You, on the other hand, look truly awful. You should be in bed, not running around out here. You can hardly walk on that leg."

Ryan moved a step closer, taking in a deep breath of the heady air. "I had to talk to you . . . to try to straighten out some things . . ."

The spirit interrupted. "It's my fault you're out here instead of in the hospital where you belong. I'm sorry. I'm damn sorry. I was so busy trying to forget I was dead that I . . . I've messed up everything for you and Emily. It wasn't intentional, just . . . hell, I guess it was just habit . . ."

Craig's voice, Ryan realized now, held a strange echo. He raised a hand to stop him. "I overheard what you two were saying. No need to say it again."

Craig looked at Emily who stood unmoving under the leaves, then back at his twin. "Yes, there is reason to say it again, because I didn't say it to you. I didn't mean to cause trouble. All that's really important to me is for you to be happy, live a good life."

"Craig—"

"No, wait. Let me say what I have to say before my energy gives out. I couldn't adjust to being over on this side because you were grieving too much. We were still too connected. You couldn't let me go, and I couldn't release you and our life. I realized yesterday that you feel guilty for being alive when I'm not. And I feel guilty for leaving."

Ryan ingested this, and he knew Craig was right.

"So all that guilt is done and over, okay? I wised up real fast when I saw what happened yesterday . . . when I realized how alone you were because of me and I had to face the fact once and for all that I can't live here anymore. So that's it. I'm going to stop playing ghost and release you both, so you can get on with living. Not because I want to, but because I love you."

Ryan's body went stiff. "You're leaving?"

"I didn't say I was leaving. I'll be hanging around until we all have a reunion over here, which for me won't be long, but I hope it's long in earth years. Meantime, no more interfering. No more materializing. I'm moving up. I've got some stuff to learn about guardianship. Got things to do. Just remember, I'll be somewhere around if you need me. That's a promise. So go live. Have fun. Love each other."

Emily watched through a blur of tears as Craig's body began to fade. In seconds the place where he stood was filled with slivers of sunlight flicked on and off by the dancing shadows of the leaves high overhead.

"Craig?" Ryan rasped.

"He's not really gone," Emily said softly. "Just because we won't see him anymore doesn't mean he's gone."

They looked at each other in the silence of the summer afternoon. Ryan's face was streaked with tears. Emily went to him and held him and, feeling the power of her love, he allowed himself to cry.

THEY LAY side by side watching the formations in the puffy clouds overhead.

"Snowdrifts," Emily said. "Just imagine us in winter, Ryan, sledding down the hills and skating on the lake, and then snuggling up in front of a cozy fire with Sanders beside us. Wouldn't it be nice? I love the winter."

He saw the snowdrifts in the clouds, too. "Why did you say that? About winter?"

"Why? I don't know. It just came to me. Funny, huh? On such a warm summer day. The clouds, maybe."

"Winter nights by the fire with you would be...really nice." Ryan turned toward her. "Nights with the woman I love. Will you stay with me, Emily? At Wildwood?"

"Ryan . . ." She rose on one elbow and looked down at him.

He smiled up at her. "Is it true that every wandering gypsy is only searching for the fires of home?"

She nodded. "I was searching for a dream and found it. Somehow you. Where you are is home."

The tips of his fingers gently brushed her cheek. "Do you love me enough to marry me?"

Emily's heart soared. "You know I do! I've loved you for a third of my life, and I know now that it was you I loved. You remember the geode, don't you? I still have it. And every time I look at it, I remember your kiss. That was the moment I fell in love."

"So did I," Ryan said, pulling her gently toward him. His kiss was different now. Strong and sure and full of the promise of a thousand tomorrows.

Epilogue

A FIRE BLAZED in the big stone fireplace. Outside the white-paned windows, snow was falling gently, adding another powdery layer to the already white world. In her soft blue sweater and woolly slippers, Emily paced nervously.

"Why isn't he home, Sanders? He should be home by now."

She stirred the apple cider in the Crock-Pot, warming with brown sugar and melted red hots, and took down two mugs from the shelf. Restless, she poured one mug full, carried it to the living room and sank onto the sofa in front of the fire. The dog jumped up beside her and lay his head on her lap.

Staring at the flames, she saw the colors of autumn, and in the colors, the images of that magical autumn day two years ago.

"Remember, Sanders? You looked so stunning in your bow tie." She smiled. "Although obviously you didn't think so or you wouldn't have eaten it afterward."

Reaching across to the end table, she set down her warm mug and picked up the small leather album she never tired of opening. Pillywiggin looked so beautiful in its autumn splendor, with leaves falling gently from overhead. The water behind it reflected the reds and oranges and yellows of the trees that lined the lake. Everything was framed in gold.

She touched each familiar picture lovingly with her fingertips. Ryan, looking so handsome, standing under the sycamore. The Tullys, all smiles. Eve, in dusty blue lace, holding hands with the town judge, who was now her husband.And here . . . the photo of Eve displaying her gift for the groom, a needlepoint pillow she made herself: Forgiveness Is Next To Godliness. Sanders looking glum in his tie. The bride and groom stepping onto the raft decked with mums under an arch made of the vines and wildflowers of late September.

Emily sighed happily. "The fireflies were so beautiful, Sanders."

The dog raised one eyebrow. She smiled. "Or maybe they weren't fireflies, huh? Maybe they were fairies. According to Ryan, fairies love to dance at weddings. Or do you already know that? I'll bet you can see them, can't you?"

Sanders flicked an ear and yawned in the warmth of the fire. He closed his eyes in total contentment.

Emily continued looking at the photos, concentrating on the odd white glow that showed up in so many of them. The photographer had been baffled by it, but not the bride and groom.

Sanders raised his head, jumped suddenly from the couch and ran toward the kitchen just as Ryan appeared in the doorway in his stocking feet, carrying the mug she had set out for him. The room was filled with the smell of apples and cinnamon and the sound of logs crackling in the fireplace.

"You're home!" she breathed, as he bent over to kiss her. "I thought you'd never get here."

"I'm not late," he said.

"But I could barely stand the wait."

He set down his mug, gave Sanders a little scratch and sat on the sofa beside her. Emily closed the book and looked at his face, so handsome in firelight.

"I couldn't wait to tell you," she bubbled.

"Tell me what?"

"Brace yourself, darling. Are you braced?"

"*What*, Emily?"

"Twins," she said.

Ryan leaped from the sofa with a whoop of joy and pulled her up and into his arms. "Twins! Sweetheart, you're a miracle worker!"

"I think technically it's your miracle," she said, smiling.

"It's *our* miracle!" He held her tightly. "The life we have together is better than I ever imagined. I know now why I waited for you to come back to me."

He put another log on the fire, and they sat hand in hand watching the popping sparks and the rising flames. Emily leaned on her husband's shoulder. "Remember when I saw winter in the clouds of summer? Now I can see spring sunshine in the fire flames. All the colors of flowers. Let's plant flowers. On Pillywiggin, too."

"Fairies thrive around flowers," he said.

"I think Craig told me once."

Sanders, resting at their feet, raised his eyebrow again, the way he often did at the mention of fairies. He sighed, gazing dreamily into the fire.

**Women throughout time have
lost their hearts to:**

Starting in January 1996, Harlequin Temptation
will introduce you to five irresistible, sexy rogues.
Rogues who have carved out their place in history,
but whose true destinies lie in the arms of
contemporary women.

#569 *The Cowboy*, Kristine Rolofson
(January 1996)

#577 *The Pirate*, Kate Hoffmann
(March 1996)

#585 *The Outlaw*, JoAnn Ross
(May 1996)

#593 *The Knight,* Sandy Steen
(July 1996)

#601 *The Highwayman,* Madeline Harper
(September 1996)

Dangerous to love, impossible to resist!

Take 4 bestselling love stories FREE

Plus get a FREE surprise gift!

BRIDE'S BAY RESORT

UNLOCK THE DOOR TO GREAT ROMANCE AT BRIDE'S BAY RESORT

Join Harlequin's new across-the-lines series, set in an exclusive hotel on an island off the coast of South Carolina.

Seven of your favorite authors will bring you exciting stories about fascinating heroes and heroines discovering love at Bride's Bay Resort.

Look for these fabulous stories coming to a store near you beginning in January 1996.

Harlequin American Romance #613 in January
Matchmaking Baby by Cathy Gillen Thacker

Harlequin Presents #1794 in February
Indiscretions by Robyn Donald

Harlequin Intrigue #362 in March
Love and Lies by Dawn Stewardson

Harlequin Romance #3404 in April
Make Believe Engagement by Day Leclaire

Harlequin Temptation #588 in May
Stranger in the Night by Roseanne Williams

Harlequin Superromance #695 in June
Married to a Stranger by Connie Bennett

Harlequin Historicals #324 in July
Dulcie's Gift by Ruth Langan

Visit Bride's Bay Resort each month wherever
Harlequin books are sold.

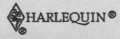

HARLEQUIN ®

BBAYG

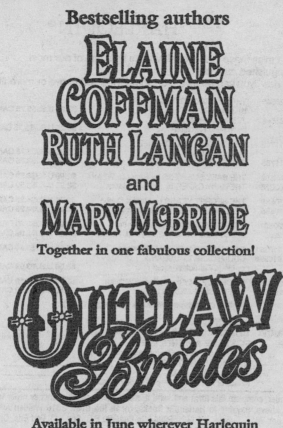

HARLEQUIN®

Don't miss these Harlequin favorites by some of our most distinguished authors!
And now, you can receive a discount by ordering two or more titles!

HT #25645	THREE GROOMS AND A WIFE by JoAnn Ross	$3.25 U.S./$3.75 CAN. ☐
HT #25648	JESSIE'S LAWMAN by Kristine Rolofson	$3.25 U.S./$3.75 CAN. ☐
HP #11725	THE WRONG KIND OF WIFE by Roberta Leigh	$3.25 U.S./$3.75 CAN. ☐
HP #11755	TIGER EYES by Robyn Donald	$3.25 U.S./$3.75 CAN. ☐
HR #03362	THE BABY BUSINESS by Rebecca Winters	$2.99 U.S./$3.50 CAN. ☐
HR #03375	THE BABY CAPER by Emma Goldrick	$2.99 U.S./$3.50 CAN. ☐
HS #70638	THE SECRET YEARS by Margot Dalton	$3.75 U.S./$4.25 CAN. ☐
HS #70655	PEACEKEEPER by Marisa Carroll	$3.75 U.S./$4.25 CAN. ☐
HI #22280	MIDNIGHT RIDER by Laura Pender	$2.99 U.S./$3.50 CAN. ☐
HI #22235	BEAUTY VS THE BEAST by M.J. Rogers	$3.50 U.S./$3.99 CAN. ☐
HAR #16531	TEDDY BEAR HEIR by Elda Minger	$3.50 U.S./$3.99 CAN. ☐
HAR #16596	COUNTERFEIT HUSBAND by Linda Randall Wisdom	$3.50 U.S./$3.99 CAN. ☐
HH #28795	PIECES OF SKY by Marianne Willman	$3.99 U.S./$4.50 CAN. ☐
HH #28855	SWEET SURRENDER by Julie Tetel	$4.50 U.S./$4.99 CAN. ☐

(limited quantities available on certain titles)

	AMOUNT	$
DEDUCT:	**10% DISCOUNT FOR 2+ BOOKS**	$
ADD:	**POSTAGE & HANDLING** ($1.00 for one book, 50¢ for each additional)	$
	APPLICABLE TAXES**	$_____
	TOTAL PAYABLE	$_____
	(check or money order—please do not send cash)	

To order, complete this form and send it, along with a check or money order for the total above, payable to Harlequin Books, to: **In the U.S.:** 3010 Walden Avenue, P.O. Box 9047, Buffalo, NY 14269-9047; **In Canada:** P.O. Box 613, Fort Erie, Ontario, L2A 5X3.

Name:_____

Address: _____ City:_____

State/Prov.:_____ Zip/Postal Code:_____

**New York residents remit applicable sales taxes.
 Canadian residents remit applicable GST and provincial taxes.

HBACK-AJ3